SCANDALOUS

SECRETS IN THE PULPIT

THE FINALE

A Novel by

K. Blaze

To submit a manuscript for our review,

email us at

submissions@majorkeypublishing.com

Acknowledgments

First and foremost, I would like to thank my Lord and Savior. If it wasn't for Him giving me the gift of writing, I wouldn't be able to do this. All praise goes to Him. My mother, who has been supportive of me since I started writing. I love you, Momma. Her encouraging words helped push me through when I felt like giving up. To Mrs. Quiana Nicole, I thank you for giving me a chance and seeing something in my writing for this opportunity. To Taneshia Ellis, my best friend, I love you for always believing in me when I didn't believe in myself. Kanesha Mitchell, I thank you for always being supportive and always keeping up with what I have going on. To each and every one of you, I say thank you from the bottom of my heart! I couldn't do this without any of you all. And to my fan base on Wattpad, I truly do thank you for reading and sharing my work.

Previously…

The Lord is my Shepard; I shall not want
He maketh me to lie down in the green pastures: he
leadeth me beside the still waters
He restoreth my soul: he leadeth me in the paths of
righteousness for his name's sake
Yea, though I walk through the valley of the shadow
of death, I will fear no evil…

Pastor Jackson Jones recited this familiar passage over and over. He didn't fear evil because he was evil. There was no way he could. He knew death faced him at every turn, but that didn't faze him. God had blessed him and had given him the power to do the things he was doing. Even in all his mess, lies and adultery, he still reigned above all.

Today was his ten-year pastoral anniversary, and the joy he felt couldn't be knocked. Things were not right on the home front, but even that didn't make him feel broken. It was all about him because he had made ten years in all his mess. Everything was hidden from his members.

They believed in him and worshiped him. He could do no wrong in their eyes. Let the majority tell it, he was a good man. He preached God's word and made a difference. His wife stood in one of the doors in the vestibule. No words were spoken. At this point, he didn't care if Sheryl talked to him or not.

"Sheryl, you don't have to say anything or show appreciation because I will still be God's chosen one," he smirked.

"You are so delusional. The devil has you fooled on so many levels. Keep on thinking you are the chosen one if you want to. You may be the chosen one, but sadly, it ain't God's chosen one," Sheryl said, shaking her head.

****

The service was going nicely. There was nothing that could break Jackson's spirit. He looked around at the larger-than-life turnout and he was grateful. Everybody loved and adored him. Almost everybody did. Jackson had accumulated so many enemies, he thought karma wouldn't come back on him.

God was about to show him just how much power the devil really had. The only thing was, the devil didn't have the power God had. It was time for Jackson to see how doing so much dirt and using God was not the way. He didn't see what was about to come his way.

Outside, Andre sat in a rental car, his gun in his lap. He had been drinking and was numb to any and everything. The parking lot was filled with cars for a man who wasn't shit. He shook his head and laughed to himself, thinking how people would fall for anything.

What he was about to do was going to hurt Summer more than anything. At this point, it didn't matter because he had already chosen the devils side. Nothing made sense anymore. His life didn't make sense anymore. He was feeling that deep depression he felt years ago. He would rather be dead than alive. Dealing with the hurt of losing was all he knew.

Andre wanted to blame God but he realized he couldn't do that because God wasn't about killing and destroying. Jackson had destroyed everything, and if he wasn't stopped, he could continue to destroy everything.

Tears streamed down his face as he thought of his parents' smiling faces the last time he saw them.

Andre stepped out of his car in all black. He was so focused on getting inside the church, he didn't know that someone in all black had entered on the other side of the church. He made his way up the stairs and walked in with his gun tucked in his waistband.

He could hear Jackson talking and Andre's blood boiled. Just as he was about to walk inside, he heard a female stand and say she needed to make an announcement.

"I have an announcement to make!" a female voice rang out.

Andre waited and listened to see what the female was going to say. It didn't take long for the woman to begin talking.

"Good afternoon, everybody, I just want to make a quick little announcement." She looked around at everyone as she walked down the aisle, holding a paper in her hand.

Andre stepped inside then. He needed to see what was about to go down before he pulled the trigger. He walked in and Jackson's eyes widened. Jackson knew something was about to go down and now he realized why he kept reciting the 23rdPsalms.

Everyone looked at Camille as she walked down the aisle. Sheryl looked at her and wondered what was going on. She finally stopped right in front of the church. She looked out at everyone before she finished saying what she needed to say.

"Many of you are wondering what I'm doing here or who I am. I will get to that in a few minutes. It's funny because, in all this crowd, I still see a few familiar faces and boy I tell you, I didn't know so many of you were married," she laughed.

Summer knew who she was and why she was there. Any other time, she would try and take up for her father, but it was time for the sheets to be pulled back on him and what he had been doing. Oddly, nobody stopped Camille or tried to put her out.

"I'm Camille, and I'm a stripper at Blue Diamond's. A lot of you men here are familiar with that strip club. Anyway, what you may not be familiar with is that your loving and devoted pastor is the owner of that club and he frequents often. Anyway, I just came to let you know that Pastor Jackson Jones ain't the man he portrays to be. He has all of you fooled."

People began to whisper and mumble. People were in shock and some sat unbothered by what Camille was saying. That didn't stop her from saying what she had to say, however. She continued with what needed to be said.

"There is one last thing I need to say before I take my seat. I have been sleeping with this man and am now carrying his child. I'm two months pregnant." She laid the paper down on the table and walked back to her seat.

And uproar took place and Andre stood, pulling his gun from his waistband. Screams broke out and people yelled that he had a gun. In the midst of all the chaos, shots rang out in every direction. Oddly, none of the shots that hit Jackson came from Andre.

When Andre turned around, the person ran out of the church. Jackson was down. All attention was on him because he still had his gun in his hand. He knew then that the shooting was going to lead to him and, once again, he hadn't done it. Amongst the chaos, he knew that nobody would believe him.

His eyes met and held Summer's from afar and the evil glare and hurt in her eyes broke him. He slid his gun back into his pants and backed out of the church. Sirens could be heard close by and he knew he needed to get out of sight as soon as possible.

Father forgive me...

******

"Yea, though I walk through the valley of the shadow of death, I will fear no evil: for thou art with me; thy rod and thy staff they comfort me." Those were the last words Jackson said before his eyes fluttered closed.

Chapter One

Two Weeks Later

Detective Jonas Smith sat back and watched the news as the reporter spoke about Jackson. He hoped he was dead, but he was still alive. It angered him that he was still alive. Jackson should have been dead. What Jonas was glad for was that none of it pointed to him. The detectives were dead set on Andre Sullivan going down for the shooting of Jackson. They knew he had motive to pull the trigger.

"How long are you planning on hiding out here, Jonas?" Jerrod asked, rubbing his goatee.

"For as long as I need to. Why are you so concerned?" Jonas looked at him with narrowed eyes.

"I was just asking. What I don't understand is why you did it."

"I had my reason and that's not for you to worry about. You just make sure you keep my secret safe. There is a lot riding on me. If word gets out, then I'm good as dead," Jonas said as he stared straight ahead in deep thought.

Jerrod shook his head and walked out. Jonas did what should have been done a long time ago. This was personal for him. He knew this was the only way to make Sheryl see that she belonged to him and only him. Hell, she always had. Pastor Jackson didn't deserve her. She was a good woman and Jackson didn't appreciate the rare gem he had.

Right now, he had to lay low until everything blew over. At the right time and right place, he would show his face. The first place he was going would be to Atlanta Medical to see Jackson. It had been a while, and it was long overdue for their impromptu meeting.

****

Summer stood by her father's bed and watched his chest move up and down. She hated seeing him like this. Sadly, she knew he had brought it on himself. There hadn't been any change in the last two weeks. He was still in a coma with tubes running in and out of his body.

"Daddy, why did you let things get so far out of control?" A tear streamed down her face as she touched her father's swollen face.

"Summer."

She didn't bother to turn around. She didn't want her mother to see her crying. That's all she had been doing since she had been there. She felt her mother touch her shoulder in a consoling manner. Right then and there, she broke down in silent tears. That was the hardest thing for her to endure.

What hurt the most was that Andre was the gunman. She pulled back from her mother's embrace, wiping her eyes. "How are you holding up?"

"By the strength of God. Summer, you can't let this bring you down. What you have to realize is there are consequences for all your actions. Jackson thought that because he held the position of pastor, he was invincible. The devil knows how to play tricks on our minds and he surely knows all of our weaknesses. Even still, we have to be ahead of him by trusting in God and his word. I'm not perfect, and I fall short of God's glory just like the next, but I ask God to forgive me. Not one time did Jackson cry out to the Lord. He kept going on and on until God got tired."

"I understand, momma, God knows I do, it just hurts to see him like this. I just wish I knew the full story behind all of this. Then there is the fact that Andre is the one who caused me this pain." Summer shook her head as she turned back to her father.

Sheryl sighed because she knew she had to tell her the whole story. She really didn't know who her father was. All she thought she knew was he had a hand in a large drug ring, but there were so many pieces to this puzzle. Her heart went out to Andre because his parents' lives had been taken all over false information, which was a setup.

"Summer, I know you may not want to hear this right now, but I think you need to go talk to Andre. You both need each other. You have to stop and think about how many other people had guns and shots rang out from different directions. Andre wasn't the only gunman. Those bullets that pierced your father could have come from anyone," Sheryl said, giving her a keen stare.

Summer looked at her mother and could see the tiredness in her eyes. She could see so much pain and it was obvious that she had been strong for too long. In spite of all that Jackson had done, she was still right by his side. Summer could also tell that she was hiding some things, too. For now, she would let it go. Soon, she would have to find out what was going on.

"Momma, I'm going to try to get some rest. We really have a lot to talk about. There are some things I need to know and there are some things you need to know as well." She grabbed her mother's hand, giving her a warm smile that she honestly didn't feel.

"We will soon. I love you."

"I love you, too, momma."

As soon as her daughter left, she turned to her husband. She had been through so much with him. By God's grace, she was still standing and she was thankful for that. At this point, she didn't know if Jackson would pull through. If he did, she was filing for divorce. She had fought a good fight, but now, Sheryl was letting go and letting God. She knew this was God's way of opening her eyes and she prayed it opened Jackson's.

Chapter Two

Summer pulled up to her condo to find Lauren standing outside her house. She rolled her eyes because she wasn't in the mood for any drama today. Summer sat there and stared at her through her window. Sighing, she got out of her car and walked towards her door.

"What are you doing here, Lauren?"

"I wanted to talk to you."

"There really isn't anything to talk about." Summer turned and looked at her.

"Summer, I'm sorry. I never me—"

"Don't you dare stand there and say you never meant for any of this to happen. You and I both know you did. Lauren, I have known you since we were little. After your parents were killed in that car crash, you just didn't give a damn. What's hard for me to get past is the fact that you spent nights and weekends at our house. My mother took you in and treated you like her own, but you repay her by sleeping with her husband, someone who should have been a father figure to you. You weren't sorry when you were with my father, knowing it would hurt me and my mother, so don't come here now talking about you sorry. The only thing you are sorry about is your hot ass getting caught. Now do me a favor and get off my doorstep!" she yelled, trying to control the tears that were slowly falling.

Lauren took one look at her before walking away with tears of her own. Summer let herself in the house and broke down. She was down on her knees, crying for her father, mother, and even for Andre. Her mother was right, she needed him like she needed her next breath. As she cried, she felt a presence behind her. Summer looked up through tear-filled eyes and saw Andre standing there.

"Andre?"

"Baby, a nigga sorry. I want you to know that even though I was there in the back with my gun, it wasn't my bullets that pierced him. Everything was happening so fast, and bullets were flying from all directions. All I can tell you is that it was somebody behind me who fired their gun several times, then they took off. I'm not sure if it was a male or female because they had on all black and they made sure their face was unidentifiable."

Summer didn't say anything as she looked up into

his worried face. She could tell he had been going through it just as she had. Without a word, Andre scooped Summer up and took her over to the couch, placing her in his lap. He held her as she cried into his chest. He hated seeing her in such a state.

"Summer, you know I care so much about you and I'm here for you through it all. I know shit ain't gon' be easy but I don't run from a damn thing. We in this shit together." He rubbed her back in circles.

Andre's ringing phone brought their moment of peace to an end. He dug into his pocket and pulled out his phone. When he saw who was calling, he mentally rolled his eyes. Summer took one look at the screen and quickly got out of Andre's lap. She wiped her eyes and looked at him with questioning eyes.

"So why is Camille calling you? Matter fact, why would you still be communicating with the whore? There really isn't any reason you should still be talking to the homewrecker anyway," Summer said with hella attitude.

Andre sighed. "I don't know why because she should be at work. I gave her a job keeping up with the inventory of what comes in."

Summer looked at him like he was crazy. She stood and walked into the kitchen. Andre came in and watched her as she moved around the kitchen. He knew she was pissed. She really didn't have a reason to be. Camille wasn't someone he was interested in. He was just doing her a favor, nothing more, nothing less.

"So you just gon' give a nigga the silent treatment?" He stepped behind her.

"Why would you give her a job, Andre? Let her work the pole like she was doing when she met my father. There is something about her I don't like. Hell, if she was messing with a married man, a pastor at that, then she wouldn't have any problems hopping on you," she said, turning around to stare into his eyes.

"You know what? I don't even know why you are here. We are not together. In all honesty, I shouldn't even be talking to you because, even if it wasn't your bullets that tore through my father, you had plans to kill him."

"I had every fucking right! He killed my parents. What did you think was gon' happen, Summer? You thought we were gon' sing hymns and have prayer meetings? Two innocent lives were taken all because your father didn't give a fuck. If I had to do it all over again, I would do it again. I don't even know why the hell I came here. You are apparently still stuck on stupid," he spat with so much venom, it could have killed Summer.

Without saying another word, he turned on his heels and left out. He couldn't believe that after everything, she was still holding it against him that he had every intention of killing Jackson. God must have been on his side because, according to the news, he was still fighting for his life. Andre looked at Summer's condo one last time before pulling off.

It made no sense to Andre that he was suffering for the sins of Summer's father. He saw that it was going to take a lot more to make her understand that her father didn't give a shit about her. All Jackson cared about was himself, and he bet money if he survived, nothing would change. He would still be the same jackass.

Chapter Three

Jackson laid in the hospital bed, and, although in a coma, his brain activity was functioning well. He could see all the shit he had done that was good and all he had done that was bad. Jackson was in a dark place and he wanted to be in the light. He felt all alone and he feared he would be alone for a long time. At this point, he wished he was dead.

"Jackson?"

He looked around and saw a bright light at the end of a dark tunnel. There was no one there. He couldn't see anyone, but he could feel a cool wind making the hairs on his arms rise. Jackson was terrified as he made his way to the end of the tunnel. The light was so bright, it was almost blinding.

"Is anybody there?" he asked in a trembling voice.

"I have always been here. You just chose to leave me."

Hearing the voice of God had Jackson's insides quivering. He couldn't believe that he was actually in a dark place with light at the end of the tunnel. This was like something out of a movie. His pulse raced a mile a minute.

25

"Why do you fear me now when you didn't fear me when you were busy sinning against me? Now you fear me only because you now know I have all power."

"God, please forgive me!" Jackson yelled with tears in his eyes.

In the blink of an eye, the light at the end of the tunnel revealed his father, Jackson Jones Sr. He was a renowned pastor of Greater Emmanuel. At one point, he was in the drug game but gave it all up when God called him to preach. Even when he did, Jackson still stayed out in the streets, hustling even after becoming a pastor.

"Son, I'm disappointed in you. You allowed the devil to take control when God is the only one who should have control. Greed got in the way and your brother did, too. That's why he ended up dead. You made a mockery of the church and, most importantly, God. The devil really had your mind, son."

Jackson looked at his father as he slowly faded away. His mother was waiting at the end of the light and waved. "May God be with you," his mother said as she disappeared.

"God, why have you forsaken me!"

The last thing Jackson wanted to see was the face of Andre's parents. No words were exchanged as they stared at each other. The whole point was to have their faces etched in his mind. They weren't the only ones Jackson had killed, but there was something about seeing them that caused guilt and sorry to wash over him. As he was about to say something, they disappeared.

The floor of the tunnel opened and he fell into the pits of hell. He could hear the horrid screams of people calling out to God. The pungent smell of burning flesh filled his nostrils. The heat of the flames where people burned was hotter than any human could stand. The further Jackson went, crying souls reached out to him.

"We meet again."

Jackson turned and was met with the evil face of Satan. Instead of fearing him, he was angered. If it weren't for him, he wouldn't be in this predicament now. He was to blame for him falling prey. Jackson was no fool, he knew Satan had power, he just didn't have power God had. God had all power.

"Why would you do this to me?"

"You wanted it, Jackson. You liked thinking you were in charge and actually had power. Truth be told, you were weak. I had to find a fool who was willing to get their hands dirty and that was you. Instead of being hungry for God's word, you were hungry for money and power. You had a choice in all this. You knew what you wanted because I am always good at persuading," Satan laughed.

A voice crying out got Jackson's attention. Hearing his brother's voice cry out almost brought him to his knees. At that moment, he didn't want to end up like Jordan. At this point, he didn't know what God had in store for him. Without warning, a ring of fire encased him. The heat was so intense, it would practically melt someone's skin off without being touched by the flame. Hell was not where he wanted to end up. There was a lot he needed to clean up if God would allow.

In his mind, he wanted to go the right way, but only time would tell. One thing for sure, God knew his heart. He could simply be running off emotions. His eyes wouldn't open, and he fought, trying to get out the darkness. It was odd that he was trying to come out of a dark place when he had been living in a dark place for so long.

A figure stood over his body with a smirk on their face. In due time, things would go according to plan. Pastor Jackson didn't realize all his sins were going to cause a world of hurt. They knew they couldn't stay long, but they had to see for themselves that Jackson was bedridden.

"In time, my dear friend, we will be face to face." The person eased out, looking around to make sure they weren't detected.

As they made their way out of the hospital, they received an incoming call.

"Hello?"

"Where the hell are you?"

"Give me fifteen, Camille, and I will be there." They hung up and headed to where they knew she would be.

Chapter Four

Lauren rushed inside the café, mentally and emotionally distraught. Lauren had lost her best friend behind living it up with her father. If she could do things all over again, she would have never gotten involved with Jackson. At this point, she hated to admit it, but she hoped he died.

She felt he didn't deserve to live. He was lower than any amount of dirt. Hell, she was, too. As she took a seat to wait for Jerrod, she noticed Sheryl walk in. It ate her up that she had done that to someone who had been there for her when her parents were killed. When she saw Sheryl approaching, her heart rate sped up.

"Hey, Lauren, I really haven't had a chance to talk to you. In fact, I really haven't seen you. Is everything okay with you?" Sheryl asked, tucking a strand of hair behind her ear.

Lauren nervously licked her lips as she stared at the woman who had been nothing but nice to her. She felt like shit for the things she had been doing. She couldn't stop the tears that fell atop her folded hands that were placed on the table. She was officially broken.

"Lauren, what's going on with you?" Sheryl asked in a concerned tone.

"I'm not the person you thought me to be. I have done a lot of things I am not proud of. Sheryl, I am so sorry for hurting you. That was never my intention." She wiped the tears as they poured from her gray eyes.

"Lauren, what are you talking about?" Sheryl sat back in her seat with narrowed eyes.

"I was sleeping with your husband and I have been for the last couple of years. I'm so so—"

WHAP!

Sheryl leaned over and smacked the holy fire out of her. Lauren looked stunned beyond belief. She held her face, knowing that due to her complexion, there would be a red mark. The look of hurt and anger made Lauren feel even worse.

"Now it makes perfect sense. You started becoming distant, but I just thought it had to do with you and Jerrod. How could you? Why would you even go that route, Lauren? You knew he was my husband and your best friend's father. You have no respect for yourself or the sanctity of marriage whatsoever. I hope it was worth it." Sheryl stood, looking around the café and noticed people were watching the scene. With her head held high, Sheryl walked out as if nothing had happened.

As soon as she got to the car, she broke down. She had been so strong for so long and she just couldn't do it anymore. The first thing she was going to do was see a divorce lawyer. There was no way she could go on living a lie. Things had changed when Jordan had practically begged Jackson to get deep in the game. For a while, Jackson was against it until finally, Jordan won him over, and the rest was history. Jackson had so many secrets and she was left looking like a damn fool. She knew of his drug dealings, but all the other stuff was a blow like never before. Then, he had gone and gotten someone pregnant. It was entirely too much.

Dear Lord, give me strength!

****

Andre decided to go to his club. He wanted to make sure things were running smoothly. Then there was the fact that his mind was filled with thoughts of Summer. He wished she could see things his way. As he made his way inside, he saw Camille behind the bar. He tried his best to breeze by, but she wasn't having it.

"Dre," Camille yelled, getting his attention

"What, Camille? I don't have time for your bullshit."

"I just wanted to know why you didn't answer my call. I called you a few hours ago," she said as she folded her arms across her chest.

"Camille, let's get two things clear. One, you are not my fucking keeper, and two, I don't answer to you. I gave you a job and your job does not consist of worrying about what I do. Now, if you want to keep this job, stay in your lane." He glared at her, leaving her with a stunned look.

Andre made his way into his office and took a seat behind his desk. He had so much on his mind. Things with him and Summer would never be on track as long as Jackson was in the picture. He wished Summer could have been the daughter of someone else. This shit was beyond complicated. If he hadn't fallen in love with her in such a short time, it would be easy to walk away from it all.

A knock sounded on his office door. For a minute, he just stared at the door, not wanting to be bothered. Taking a deep breath, he finally acknowledged the person on the other side of his door. "Come in!" his deep voice boomed.

When he looked up, who he knew had to be Summer's mother walked in. She was a beautiful woman who looked to be in her later thirties or early forties. They stared at each other and Andre could tell she had so much to say. He wasn't sure if he was ready to hear it, especially if it was about her no-good ass husband.

"Andre, I know you are probably wondering why I am here," she said as she made her way into the office, closing the door.

"Listen, Mrs. Jo—"

"There is no need to apologize. If anything, I need to apologize to you for all the grief that has been thrown your way. I don't condone any of what my husband has done. In fact, he got what he deserved."

Andre leaned back in his high back leather chair, staring at Mrs. Jones. He was surprised. He just knew she was going to be on her husband's side regardless. Now that really piqued his interest. It was obvious she wasn't there for his shit, either. "So, what is it you want to talk to me about?" He narrowed his light brown eyes at her.

"I wanted you to know that I did everything in my power to make sure you got the closure you needed. I knew for years that my husband was off. Honestly, I just brushed it off, hoping he would turn his evil ways. I prayed constantly for him to turn his ways. Once my daughter started seeing you, I knew things were going to hit the fan."

"What are you saying, Mrs. Jones?"

"I'm saying I don't blame you for the actions you took, and if it had to be done all over again, I would understand. I knew I had to give you the information you needed in order for you to find closure, even though I know it still hurts. Your parents were good people."

"What information are you talking about?"

Mrs. Jones sighed. "The manila envelope that was left on your doorstep was left by me. I paid Detective

Smith two hundred grand for that leather glove. See, he was in on helping Jackson back then, but money talks, and he felt he owed me that."

"What th—"

"Let me finish." She raised her hand to stop Andre from talking.

"The man I sent you to get the glove analyzed is your uncle."

Andre stood from his seat and stared at Sheryl as if she had lost her mind. There was no way Marshall Lyndon was his uncle. He never knew his father to have a brother. Shit wasn't adding up, and because of Jackson, things were only spiraling out of control more.

"Listen, I don't know what kind of games you are playing, but I know Marshall isn't any kin to me."

"I know this is a lot to take in, Andre, but just trust me. Your father and Marshall didn't have the same mother. His mother gave him up at birth."

Andre had so much going through his mind. Hell, he had so much going on. He and Summer weren't on good terms. He was being watched as well as questioned for the attempted murder of Jackson. Andre had been arrested, but there wasn't a reasonable cause to detain him since there were too many other people at the scene. Sheryl was on some other shit. Times like this, he really wished he could be with Summer.

Andre had heard enough for the day. "Mrs. Jones, this all too much for me. If you would see yourself out." He dismissed her.

Sheryl stared at him for a minute and finally turned to leave. This wasn't over because there was so much he needed to know. At the right time, things would come together and hopefully, things would turn around. Summer and Andre were blessings to each other, in spite of all the hell Jackson had put them both through.

God had everything under control because He had all power. Things would come together in His time and she believed that some people were going to feel God's wrath. As she walked towards her car, her cell phone rang. She looked at the screen and saw that it was the hospital. Taking the call as she opened the car door, she listened to the nurse tell her she needed to get there. Ending the call, she started her car and pulled out from Andre's spot. Hopefully, it wasn't any more bad news. At least Sheryl prayed it wasn't.

Chapter Five

Jackson laid there with his eyes open. He stared straight ahead with so many emotions flooding him. Jackson had never felt so alone in all his years. He was fooled by the tricks of the devil, thinking he was something when he was nothing. There were so many wrongs he wished he could right.

Sheryl had been by his side for all twenty-four years and had supported him, yet she would tell him when he was wrong. He had done so much, there was no way God was going to show him favor. Jackson was thankful that God had brought him back from that dark place he was in.

He still had his chest tube in and oxygen had now replaced the respirator. His body was in so much pain. Everything that had happened was because of that nigga Andre. He prayed Summer wasn't still dealing with him after what had happened. If so, he had to go. In the midst of his mind rants, the door opened, and there stood his gorgeous wife.

They stared at each other without saying anything.

Both of them had their minds in different places. Sheryl was thinking how much of a blessing it was going to be to walk away and stay away, and Jackson was thinking of ways to keep his wife and make things better.

They had met when Sheryl was soon to turn fourteen. She was the good girl around the way, and since he had been having sex since the age of twelve, he knew Sheryl wasn't with it. At the age of fourteen, she ended up getting pregnant and her parents were livid. They were too young to get married, but as soon as they hit eighteen, they were married. His parents were livid as well, but their faith in God allowed them to love and support them all the same. That was one of the reasons Jackson was so hard on her because he didn't want her ruining her life at a young age.

"I can't believe you are here. Honestly, I didn't think you would be," Jackson said in a raspy voice.

"Trust me, I thought about it. So, how are you feeling?"

"I feel bad, but not just physically, mentally and emotionally also." He looked at her with sad eyes.

At one time, those eyes would make her weak.

Now when she looked at her husband, she felt disgusted. It was amazing how much a man could do to a woman to make her feel repulsed. "I hope this incident has taught you a lesson."

Jackson looked away because he really didn't know if it had. Deep down, he was still Jackson and he felt he still had some power. He knew his silence was golden and his wife already knew the answer to what she asked. Jackson didn't think he would be as bad as he was before because God had blessed him to see the light of day.

"You know what, Jackson, you don't even have to answer that because I see that nothing has really changed. I'm glad to see you are doing well. Summer should be here later," Sheryl said, walking out and leaving a stunned Jackson.

He wondered had any of his church members been to see him. Chico and Spin were his right hands and he wondered if they were holding the church down as they should have been. Oddly, Sheryl hadn't even mentioned the church and that made him wonder what the hell was going on. Something was definitely off.

He closed his eyes to get some rest when his room door opened. When he looked over, he saw that it was Camille. He wondered what the hell she wanted. "Camille, because of you, I'm in this predicament," he said, wincing in pain.

"Really? You want to go there? When you was laid up with me, you wasn't worried about nothing being my fault. Hell, your fake ass wasn't worried about nothing, but since you wanna play these blame games, just know I will have the last laugh. Oh, and I'm glad to see you *pulled* through," Camille smirked.

Jackson looked at her like she had lost her mind. Something was definitely off with her and he was going to have to be on his A game. He knew it was going to take him some time in order to keep an eye on her. God hadn't spared his life for no reason. He was grateful and he couldn't wait until he was strong enough to get back on the scene. Patience was of the essence and he had to pray for it in order to make it through.

Chapter Six

Two months later

Jackson was back on his feet and moving around. The church was still in full force, but he had lost a lot of members. Even still, he had a good sized congregation. Regardless of what happened, he still had his beloved followers. Spin had been holding down the fort and he had done a good job. Now it was time for him to get back to it. Things with his family were off and he couldn't blame anybody but himself. He believed that with the Lord on his side, he would make it through.

His wife had moved out when she could've stayed. Summer hadn't been around, and he didn't even know if she had been the whole time he was stowed away in the hospital. He still had eyes and ears on the street and word was, Andre and Summer weren't communicating. At least he'd gotten what he wanted, or so he thought.

The doorbell jarred Jackson from his thoughts. He slid his hands in his dress pants and headed down the steps. Not bothering to look out the peephole, he opened the door to find Detective Jonas Smith standing there. He couldn't understand what the hell he was doing there, considering he hadn't heard from him in a very long time. Something had to be up with Jonas.

"What are you doing here? I told you after I paid you that money for helping me cover my tracks we were done. So, tell me, why are you here?" Jackson asked as he folded his arms across his massive chest.

Jonas smirked. "See, my friend, that's where you are wrong. We have a lot of business. I hold a lot of valuable information and I think you would like to be in on this."

Jackson frowned, unsure if he wanted to believe him or not. Thinking for a moment, he decided to let him in. Jonas looked around with jealousy laced in his dark-brown stare. He felt as though he had been cheated out of having all that Jackson had. In time, he would have that and more, plus his beautiful wife. Jonas just had to play both ends against the middle to get everything he wanted.

"So, what is it you need to talk to me about?" Jackson leaned against the kitchen counter and waited for Jonas to speak.

"It's about your wife. Let's just say she had a hand in you being shot."

Jackson laughed as if Jonas were joking. When he saw how serious he was, he quickly stopped laughing. "What the hell do you mean my wife played a part in me being shot?"

"Jackson, money talks and bullshit walks. With that being said, your wife paid me a helluva lot of money for the evidence I had supposedly gotten rid of. Fortunately for me, I kept it as insurance for the day I may need it."

Rage filled Jackson like never before. It was just like the day he found out his brother had been killed. His mind warred with his soul. Jonas didn't see the hit coming, but he damn sure felt when blood gushed from his mouth. Unfazed, Jonas wiped the blood from his mouth with the back of his hand.

"Don't get mad because your pretty little wife got tired of your bullshit. You are supposed to be a man of the cloth, yet you out here with twenty different spirits controlling you. I'm not a religious man by any means, although I do know you reap what you sow, and you, my friend, will do so." Jonas smirked and turned on his heels because his work was done.

Jackson was now thinking, and his line of thinking was all wrong. He couldn't believe his own wife would sell him out like that. There were so many questions roaming in his head, it didn't make any sense. All he could think was somebody had to die because this wasn't the way things were supposed to go.

I guess the old Jackson never died...

Chapter Seven

Lauren sat at the doctor's office, nervous. She felt she needed to get a check-up because Jackson had been around the block. She began to pray to God as she waited for the doctor to come back into his office. *Lord, I know I haven't been the best person and I have done a lot of things that weren't pleasing to Your hearing or sight. I lost sight of a lot of things, chasing the wrong things when I should have been chasing You. Lord, please just bless me and keep me in Your care. In Jesus' name, I pray. Amen,* she prayed silently.

No sooner than she got through praying, the door opened and the doctor walked in, flipping pages in a chart. He looked at Lauren and smiled weakly. "Ms. Lyles, I don't quite know how to tell you this."

"Tell me what?" She furrowed her brows.

"You are HIV positive."

"No! You have to be wrong about this, doctor. There is no way!" she screamed as tears streamed down her face.

"I'm sorry, Ms. Lyles. There are anti-retroviral

drugs I can prescribe to slow the process of the disease. Even though you don't want to hear this, there are people who live normal lives. You don't have to give up," the doctor tried to reassure.

Lauren was numb. She couldn't believe this was her fate. Not even five minutes ago, she had prayed to God to take care of her. She felt God hadn't heard her prayer. The tears wouldn't stop as she cried out. She was only twenty-four years old and this was her punishment. Not only was her life ruined, but so were innocent people's lives who had nothing to do with her choices. Sheryl's life was in jeopardy and that cut her like a knife.

"What am I going to do? I don't even know who I could've gotten it from." Lauren started going crazy. She stood and started tearing the doctor's office apart. He managed to press the button for security, and they rushed in and grabbed Lauren, taking her away as she fought and screamed. Lauren had no idea Camille was on the same floor and saw what was happening. Camille already knew what was going on because she had been HIV positive for the last few years. She was raped outside of Jackson's strip club and the person who raped her was HIV positive. So, when she slept with him, she had to play the victim role to make it look good.

Jackson was the devil himself and he had taught everyone around him how to be devilish. Things were working in her and her brother, Detective Smith's favor. The beauty of it was, no one knew the two were related. Things were getting better and better. Everything she desired would soon be hers. If she could only get Andre to fall into the palm of her hands.

Camille walked out, rubbing her stomach. She felt like things would finally work in her favor. It had been a long time coming and she deserved to have the best. She didn't care at what cost, nor did she care who got hurt. It was her time, and she was glad things were finally looking up. She hoped like hell nothing happened to mess up what she and Jonas had going on.

Jackson just didn't understand that he was still under the radar, and just because he pulled through that time, didn't mean he would the next. Eventually, he would get his. Every dog had its day and he would soon have his.

He used people and he used his power as a pastor to get over. She was far from a saint, but karma was real and *Pastor* Jackson Jones had his dose of karma around the corner, he just didn't see it yet. His perfect world was about to become a disaster and he wasn't going to know what hit him.

It had just begun and it felt good to feel powerful for a change. Jackson wasn't the only one who felt like they had the power. Everyone did. It was up to that individual to use it in a way that would be beneficial, and she was damn sure making sure she was doing so. She got chills just thinking about it. Camille smiled, walking out of the doctor's office.

Chapter Eight

Summer stood and looked around her downtown makeup boutique. She had put her heart and soul into her boutique but it no longer felt the same. She and Lauren were no longer friends and it hurt to know that Lauren had hurt her, and most of all, her mother. Summer had isolated herself from everyone, including her father. She knew he was out of the hospital, but she really didn't have words for him.

She was hurt about what had happened, and Summer felt her father wasn't going to change. All it would take is something to take him back to that dark place and he would go back to being the Jackson everyone knew. Sad to say, but she was blind to who he had been all those years. It was sad that one man had caused so much pain and had done so much dirt. Today was going to be her last day in Atlanta. It was time for a change, and she was heading to Miami.

Summer had been busy finalizing things for her move. She had been so busy, she hadn't talked to her mother, but today she would. Andre had been reaching out to her for the last month or so but she still didn't want to deal with him. It was so hard because she loved him with everything in her. Things were just a mess right now and it wasn't their time.

Everything had been packed and the movers were moving everything out. Summer stood, looking around her building, not believing it had come to this. She slid her hands in the back pockets of the black distressed jeans she was wearing. She turned around, and when she did, Andre stood there, looking finer than any man had a right to.

He was rocking all black and had a fresh cut. His goatee was trimmed neatly and his rich caramel skin was flawless. There was pain written all over his handsome face. Seeing that tugged at Summer's heart. She didn't know what to say. She felt she needed to say something, but she wasn't sure that would be the best thing to do at the moment.

"Andre, what are you doing here?" she asked, tucking her hair behind her ear.

"I came to talk to you. I miss you and I need you," he said, taking a step closer, towering over Summer.

"Andre, now really isn't a good time."

"Why, because you are leaving?"He looked around the almost empty boutique.

Summer didn't say anything as she nervously chewed her bottom lip. She hoped to have been gone before anyone could reach her. All she wanted to do was talk to her mother before she left and be done with Atlanta. "Andre, please don't do this, not now. And yes, I'm leaving. It's time for a change. In fact, it's for the best. I hope you can understand that."

"Where are you going?" He rubbed his hand across his waves as he watched her.

"That you don't need to know, Andre. Besides, I think it's for the best."

Andre narrowed his eyes as he stared at Summer's beautiful face. He loved her more than anything, and all of it was torn apart by one man. There had to be a way for them to work through everything because it was as if it ended before it started. "Summer, what the hell is running going to solve? The fact will always remain of what your father caused. Also, you leaving isn't going to change the fact that we love each other."

"Andre, just let me go and you live your life. I'm sure Camille would love to be a part of your world." She rolled her eyes dramatically.

"Dammit! Summer, I don't want her or any other woman. I want you. I don't care about what's going on around us. All we need is each other." Andre stepped in and caressed her cheek.

Summer reached up and placed her hand on top of his wrist. She stared into his beautiful eyes and knew that no matter what, he would always have her heart. Right now, she needed to get her life together and have some time to herself. The longer she stayed, the more her heart would break. Things were just too much and she knew that before they got better, they would get worse.

"Andre, I love you with all my heart, God knows I do, but right now, I just need to move on from here. Just give me some time, and if it's meant to be, God will bring us back together." She leaned in and kissed him, causing him to grab her, pulling her close.

"I love you, Andre," she whispered against his lips

as she slid out of his embrace.

Andre stood there and let her go, knowing in his heart he didn't want to. He knew that he had to, but he believed they would be together. They were meant to be together and no matter the storm that had turned their world upside down, he had faith. He stood there a moment longer and decided he had business he had to handle. What Summer failed to realize was that he would find her. They were going to have their real and fair chance. It didn't matter what Summer had to say about it.

Andre made his way out of her empty boutique and headed to his car. He had a feeling that some shit was going to pop off. It was a gut feeling, and usually, his gut feelings were right. Somehow, he figured Jackson would be with his bullshit sooner or later. All hell was soon to break loose once Jackson found out about Marshall Lyndon, who was Andre's father half-brother.

The ringing of his phone brought him from his thoughts. He grabbed his phone from his cup holder and looked at the screen. Andre rolled his eyes when he saw that it was Camille. She was doing the most and he didn't want shit to do with her. He knew what she was about and he didn't want any parts of that. He declined her call and started his car. In a few weeks, he would take a trip to Miami and handle some business. He had even thought about moving there.

The way things were going, he had nothing to lose by moving there. He had his restaurant and he could open another club. The more he thought about it, the more the idea sounded better. Hell, his heart was gone with Summer, so there was really no point in staying in the A.

Chapter Nine

"Let us give God some glory and let us give God some praise!" Jackson said, standing behind the pulpit.

People stood, giving God glory, waving their hands in the air. Amens rang out along with, "Praise God." The spirit was high and Jackson was on cloud nine. He looked out into his congregation and his heart sunk not seeing his wife or his daughter. Shaking it off, he continued to urge the people to praise God.

"I don't know about you, but God has been good to me. As many of you know, I went through an ordeal a couple months ago. God healed my body because there is power in the name of Jesus. Am I right about it?"

"Yeah!"

"Today I want to take you to a familiar scripture. If you would turn with me to Mark 11:24. When you have found it, let it be known by saying Amen."

"Amen."

"Mark 11:24 reads: Therefore I say unto you, What things soever ye desire, when ye pray, believe that ye receive them, and ye shall have them.

"Now what God is telling you is when you call on Him and ask, you will receive. You have to believe in your heart that He hears your prayer as well as answers it. He hears the prayers of the righteous. See, when I was laid in that hospital bed, I didn't know if I was going to come out, but God healed my body. I called on the Lord and He heard my cry," Jackson said, walking back and forth across the pulpit.

Some people in the congregation stood, lifting their hands in praise. Jackson looked back to Spin and he, too, was on his feet. Chico was on the front pew, but oddly, Jerrod wasn't there and that didn't sit well with him. He hadn't realized it until that moment. Right now, he couldn't worry about that, though. He would deal with that later.

****

Summer was now on the plane and her thoughts were everywhere. First, it was Andre, and after the conversation she had with her mother, it was worse. Her mother explained that she was the one who had given the information on Jackson killing Andre's parents. What really had her head spinning was Marshall Lyndon was Andre's uncle. That only made for more blood to be shed when they should let go and let God fight their battles.

To top it all off, her mother had filed for divorce and he would be getting the papers as early as tomorrow. She knew her father was back to preaching and he still had most of his members. A good bit left after the turmoil. They followed where God led them, not where man led them. She was glad to have escaped what was going on. Summer wanted her mother to come with her, but she understood she had to tie up loose ends.

Something in her spirit was uneasy. She had a feeling something was going to happen. Summer hated feeling the way she was. Most of the time when she had those feelings, something would happen. So much had happened and so much was going on as is, she didn't know if she could take anything else. Sometimes God allowed things to happen to open blinded eyes.

Miami was her place of peace for now, but Summer already missed Andre. She needed him, but right now, she needed this time to find inner peace from all the drama in her young life.

Chapter Ten

Jerrod sat in the darkened living area with a glass of Hennessy in his hand. He had a gun in his lap as his bloodshot eyes stared into the dark. He couldn't believe his life was gone. He hadn't even made it to thirty yet. Jerrod had gone to have a routine check-up a few days ago and he learned he was HIV positive.

Ever since he'd found out, he already knew who he had gotten it from. Lauren had played him. She had really done him dirty. Or maybe she didn't know she had the virus. However, Jerrod felt he didn't have a reason to live. God was tired of all the foolishness and had sealed his fate. Now he wondered if she had gotten it from Jackson or had she gotten it from someone else. At this point, it didn't matter because he knew for sure this was his punishment. Hell, there was no need for Jackson to know he was the one who had killed his brother. He took his drink to the head and rubbed the gun in his lap.

There's truth in the saying, you reap what you sow. He had sowed some bad seeds, and in return, he was reaping everyone. Tears streamed down his face as he thought about how this was going to be a chain reaction. He knew this was the best way to handle things. Jerrod didn't want to suffer from the HIV virus. He threw the glass against the wall and watched as it shattered the same way his heart had. All the while, he could hear a still voice. He was so hurt, he was overriding the spirit of God.

He placed the barrel of the gun up to his temple as tears continued to stream down his face. He released the safety. "Father forgive me." As soon as he said those final words, he pulled the trigger and the gun fell from his hand as his body slumped to the side. Now there was no need for anyone to come looking for him because all they would find was a dead body that couldn't give answers.

The next day

Jackson sat in his empty house with Chico and Spin. They discussed what was going on in the streets. He even told them about Jonas and his threats. They knew things were about to get out of hand, but it was nothing they couldn't handle. Nothing had changed as far as they were concerned. Jackson was going to have to get Jonas before he got him.

"So, what's the move, Jackson?" Spin asked, taking a pull from his blunt.

"We can keep tabs on him like we did with Andre and Summer," Chico added.

Jackson nodded as he sat back in his chair. He knew he handled the streets. What he couldn't get over was how his wife had betrayed him. Not only that, she had gotten the balls to leave him. She had become defiant and that was something that didn't sit well with him. After what Jonas had told him, he felt they might have had something going on.

"Jackson, where is Sheryl?, We haven't seen her much," Spin asked and Chico nodded in agreement.

Jackson was just about to answer when his doorbell rang. He stood up and walked towards the door. Looking out of his peephole, he saw a preppy black guy. He opened the door and the guy greeted him. "Jackson Jones?"

"Yeah?"

"This is for you. You've been served." The courier passed a thick envelope.

The courier turned on his heels and walked off, leaving Jackson wondering what the hell was going on. He stood in the doorway and opened the envelope. When he pulled the contents of the envelope out, he leaned into the doorframe, not believing his wife had filed for divorce. Twenty-five years she was throwing away. Anger filled his body and that made things even worse. He was already angry about Jonas, and now this.

"Yo, Jackson, you good man?" Spin asked as he walked up behind him.

"Sheryl just filed for divorce."

"Damn."

Chapter Eleven

Sheryl sat at the café around the corner from her condo. She sipped from her iced tea as she waited for her food to arrive. Jackson should have gotten the divorce papers by now, and it wouldn't be long before he started calling. He hadn't been calling that much, but she knew he would now. She was grateful for him not knowing where she lived.

It was time for a change and the change started with getting rid of the poison. That was all Jackson had been. At one point, he wasn't as mean and evil as he had been these past few years. Things changed when his father died, and then more so when Jordan was killed. She knew he thought she should have been on his side. Sadly, she had been on his side for too long, even when he was wrong.

God was giving her an out and she was taking it. She had prayed and asked God to guide her and He had. She would be forever thankful for Him opening that door. Seconds later, her meal arrived and she quickly blessed her food. When she opened her eyes, Jonas was standing over her with a smirk on his face.

"Do you mind if I join you?" Jonas flourished his hand towards the table.

"I do mind. Unfortunately, I know that isn't going to stop you from having a seat."

Jonas took a seat across from her and stared at her. She was flawless and he wanted her. The first time he laid eyes on her, he knew he had to have her. The night after her brother-in-law was killed, he thought somebody had knocked the wind out of him when he saw her. He couldn't believe she had been with Jackson as long as she had.

"So why are you sitting here, eating alone? You're too beautiful to eat alone." He smiled, revealing pearly white teeth.

Sheryl looked at him and she had to admit that he was a good looking man. He was another Jackson, though. Jonas was cocky and very arrogant. He dressed impeccably, he kept his hair cut low, and his facial hair was always on point. "I'm eating alone because I choose to stay away from men like you. I'm married to a ruthless man now, so tell me why the hell I would want to get involved with another?" She cut her smothered chicken, taking a bite.

"Touché. You know I'm a better man."

Sheryl looked at him and shook her head. Jonas was no better than Jackson. They both wanted power, and they were both greedy for money. People would think they were related. Deciding not to respond, Sheryl continued eating, only to have him watching her intently. He was starting to get on her last nerve.

"What is it you want, Jonas?"

"That's easy, Sheryl. I want you and I have since the first day I laid eyes on you," he admitted without taking his eyes off her.

Sheryl didn't know what to say. She was shocked because she had no idea. Jonas always played cool whenever in her presence. The more she looked at him, the more she saw evilness within his eyes. Jonas had a hidden agenda. As of now, she wasn't sure what it was. Sooner or later, it would reveal itself. That she was for sure. She was sure he had secrets.

"Jonas, I would say that it was good seeing you, but I'm not going to lie and say that it was. Look, I know you helped me out and I paid you quite nicely. If you are looking for anything else in return, then you are looking in the wrong direction." Sheryl stood and dropped money on the table.

"You know, Sheryl, it won't be long before Jackson comes looking for you. I mean, since he knows you were the one who played a part in him getting shot." He smirked as he always did.

"It doesn't matter to me because what's done is done. I have no reason to run or fear him. Man can only hurt me as much as I allow man to. So you telling me that has done nothing but make me trust God even more than I did. Remember, Jonas, he is the one who's losing and has lost. All his dirty deeds have cost him to lose people he supposedly cared about. Loved, even. First, it was his brother, then it was his daughter, and now me. Good day, Jonas." Sheryl walked out with her head held high.

Jonas sat there with anger flashing in his eyes. He couldn't believe Sheryl had blown him off the way she had. She was so full of herself. He couldn't stand women like her. She thought her God would protect her. Jonas felt as though he deserved her. Jackson didn't, and he never would, he was just biding his time. He had to go find his sister to see how things were going on her end. That reminded him that he hadn't seen or talked to Jerrod in a while. Something told him Jerrod had skipped town, or at least he hoped that's what it was.

Jonas stood from the table and headed out. The whole time he was walking out, he had no idea Marshall Lyndon was watching him. Jonas nor Jackson knew the hell that was about to take place in their lives. It was good that no one knew about him because he would move in silence.

"Can I get you anything else?" the young waitress asked Marshall.

"No, I'm fine. Thank you."

She nodded and headed off across the floor. Marshall was waiting for his nephew. They hadn't talked since that day he analyzed Jackson's leather glove. At the time, he didn't know Marshall was his uncle. The look on his face when he did see him was priceless. Marshall looked so much like Anthony.

Anthony's dad had paid his mistress to keep Marshall away. When he got older, he came around. Once their father stopped coming around, Marshall's mother left him without a backward glance. That was how Marshall ended up in the system. He was only seven at the time. The thing is, he was always lurking in the shadows. Even before Sheryl had gotten him the glove, he knew Jackson had something to do with the murder, he just didn't have the proof he needed at the time. The word on the street was heavy.

Marshall looked up as his nephew walked into the café. He looked so much like his father it was scary. Andre also had a lot of his mother's features as well. He watched as he scanned the crowd. Finally, his eyes landed on the table where he was located. Andre walked over with his face void of any emotions. He took a seat and stared at Marshall.

"So, you my pop's brother?" he asked with a hint of attitude.

"Yes. Look, I know this is all new and you have every reason not to believe me. My mother was paid by my father to stay away. He didn't want your grandmother Marla, to know about his infidelities. When my father stopped coming around, my mother left me at the age of seven. I ended up in the system shortly after."

"So, what are you here for now? Is it money?" Andre questioned, trying to understand.

"Dre, I have money. I keep a low profile. I have always been around since I was twenty-one. See, I kept a close eye on things. I just hate that I didn't get to have a sit down with your father before he was killed. There was so much bad blood, I knew something was bound to happen. My father had taken over the game, and when Jackson's father left the street life alone, Jackson took over. He became greedy and jealous because of the operation we had going on. Even though I was never seen much, I was always working."

"So how did you get into the forensic bullshit?"

"When I got word that my brother was killed, I knew I had to put my criminal degree to use. Nobody knew about me but select people. I make a killing doing what I do. Sheryl came to me and we had a long talk and I told her who I was. Shortly after she came to me with what I needed to help you find out who killed your parents."

Andre listened to everything he was saying. All this shit was crazy and he wished he had known his uncle sooner. "If you anything like my pops, then I know you plotting something."

"Oh, I am. I'm also watching a few people, too. Detective Smith is definitely on my radar. I have to dig up some things on him because I feel like he had reason to try and kill Jackson. First, I have to find out if he has any family members around who know him. Since nobody knows me, I'm sure I can make something happen. In the meantime, stay in touch." Marshall slid his card over to Andre.

Andre nodded and watched as Marshall stood to leave. At times like this, he wished like hell he could be wrapped up in Summer's arms. He missed her like crazy. Dwelling on it wasn't going to help matters any. He had a few days before he went to Miami. Hopefully, that would ease his troubled mind.

******

Sheryl had just gotten out of her car when she heard footsteps behind her. She quickly turned around to find Jackson standing there, looking like the devil himself. Anger flashed in his eyes. She already knew he had gotten his little surprise. The Lord was going to have to give her the strength to deal with him.

"What do you want, Jackson?"

He tilted his head to the side and stared at her. He couldn't believe she had played him to the left. "So you like disrespecting your *husband*?"

"All is fair in love and war, Jackson. You're not the only one who makes things happen."

Chapter Twelve

Jackson looked at his wife like he had never seen her before. She had changed. No longer was she the woman who went along with whatever he said or did. Sheryl had found her inner strength. He liked her being submissive, or a better term in his defense, stupid. Now he could no longer control her.

"Oh, I see that nigga Jonas got you feeling yourself."

"No, Jackson. God opened my eyes. I was living in the midst of your sin, acting like it was okay. That was never okay, husband or not. You took things too far, and now I'm doing what I should have had the strength to do a long time ago and that's leave!"

"So you think you just gonna leave me after I practically made you? You didn't have shit when I first met you. You tend to forget how you got pregnant the first time at fourteen. If it wasn't for me and my drug money, you wouldn't have the lavish life you live. How the hell you think you living in this fancy condo and driving that car? It's my damn money!" he barked.

Sheryl smirked. "See, that's what you think. Baby, I been had my own money stashed. In fact, I have been saving for years. Momma didn't raise no fool. A man like you would love to see me broke down. Jackson, you are weak. You need someone you can control because you think you are God. Guess what, though, God broke them chains and set me free from the hold you had on me. Now, if there is nothing else, from this point on, the only person you need to talk to is my lawyer." Sheryl turned on her heels and walked inside her house.

Jackson stood there, not believing what had just happened. Things were spinning out of control. Things were not supposed to go on like this. He had the power. Right at that moment, he felt God had betrayed him again. He knew when he was in his coma he had made God a promise, but promises were meant to be broken. Jackson was dumb as they came for allowing the devil to play mind games with him. His way wasn't God's way anymore, and he was soon going to learn that it was God's way or no way at all.

******

Lauren sat all alone, thinking about her life. She was only twenty-four and had done so much wrong. Now all her wrongs had caught up with her. She tried calling Jerrod but to no avail; the phone kept going to voicemail. She had a bad feeling that something was wrong. Lauren really hadn't seen him in a while, and she wondered if he had skipped town.

At times like this, she wished she had never betrayed Summer. Her life now was full of empty regrets. If she could only turn back the hands of time. Lauren looked terrible, but not because of the fact she was HIV positive. It was because she had no one in her corner and she just didn't care anymore. There was no reason she should at this point.

Lauren grabbed her keys and decided to go check on Jerrod. At some point, she was going to have to tell him about being HIV positive. She hopped in her car and started the ignition. Lauren backed out and drove in silence. It was a good thing he didn't stay too far from her. It took about fifteen minutes for her to get there. She parked and slowly got out.

Walking up to the door, she rang the bell repeatedly. After about five minutes of ringing, she decided to go around back to get the key he left under the mat. Instead of walking back around to the front of the house, she decided to let herself in from the back door. For some reason, her heart was pounding.

She let herself in and it smelled terrible. Lauren covered her nose as she trailed through. Once she got to the living area, her eyes landed on Jerrod's dead body and she puked everywhere. She knew right then that he knew and that broke her even more. Because of her hoe-ish ways, people were dying. With shaky hands, she pulled out her phone and dialed 911.

In a frantic voice, she told the dispatcher what had taken place as best as she could. Twenty minutes later, the coroner, as well as detectives, arrived. They asked her a series of questions and she answered them. She watched as they zipped his body in a black bag. This was so unreal to her and she couldn't believe it. Jerrod hadn't talked to his parents in years, and she hated to have to call them to tell them that he had committed suicide. He was estranged from his parents once he got involved in the streets. His parents were very religious people and they believed the streets weren't the place for a deacon.

Hours later, Lauren made it back home. She sat in her room after getting off the phone with Jerrod's parents. They were devastated. The sad part was, he hadn't died because of the streets. He had died because Lauren was being a hoe in the streets. She was chasing paper, thinking it was cute to sleep with a married man. It was fascinating then, but now, it was a nightmare.

"God, protect those innocent in all of my wrongdoings. Keep them covered by Your blood, especially Sheryl. She doesn't deserve any of this. Lord, I know this isn't the prayer of the righteous, but please hear my prayer, Lord. In Jesus' name, I pray. Amen."

Jerrod's funeral would be the following week and she already knew it was going to be a hard pill to swallow. Lauren laid down as tears began to flow. She had never felt so broken in all her life. It's funny how a person didn't worry or think about calling on God until they were in trouble. Living the highlife tended to make people forget about God and who He is.

Only if she had been like Summer, her life would be better. She knew it wouldn't be perfect, but it would be better than it was now. Lauren now lived with so many regrets. There was nothing she could do now. She had made her bed, so now she had no choice but to lay down in it. God was showing her that He had all power and no man on earth had the power He had. Lauren chose to worship man and not God. Since she had made that decision, she was paying for it dearly and began clinging to God more than she ever had before.

Chapter Thirteen

Today was the day of Jerrod's funeral, and of all people, Pastor Jackson Jones was doing the eulogy. The devil himself stood trying to preach somebody into heaven when he himself was on his way to hell. Before he began his sermon, a soloist by the name of Melody James began to sing "God Will Take Care of You."

Be not dismayed whatever betide
God will take care of you
Beneath His wings of love abide
God will take care of you
God will take will take care of you
Through every day all the way
(He will take care of you)
God will take care of you

As Melody sung, tears and sobs filled Greater Emmanuel. It was such a sad case because no one knew the real reason as to why Jerrod had killed himself. Lauren did and her heart broke into a million pieces as tears streamed down her face. It was too much, so she got up and ran out of the church in heart-wrenching sobs.

Outside the church, Lauren held herself as she let it all out. Still hearing Melody sing the soulful lyrics, she felt a calm she had never felt before. She knew she needed to get her life together. It didn't matter that she may not have had much time; she just felt she needed to get her house in order. Hell was not where she wanted to open her eyes, although she knew that was where she belonged. She decided that being there was a mistake and she needed to get out of there. Within minutes, Lauren left Greater Emmanuel.

"See, Brother Jerrod was a fine young man who did whatever was needed. He was a phenomenal deacon. He loved the Lord and didn't mind working for the Lord. We don't know what he was going through, therefore it isn't our place as Christians to judge." Pastor Jackson wiped his mouth as he looked down at his bible. "A familiar scripture comes to mind when I think about Deacon Jerrod. It seems that his heart may have been troubled, but John 14:1 states: Let not your heart be troubled: ye believe in God, also believe in me." A chorus of hallelujahs and Amens sounded off.

"See, God can take care of all your troubles. God doesn't put any more on you than you can bear. Jerrod lived his life for the Lord and worked diligently within Greater Emmanuel. He gave his best years to the Lord." Jackson looked down at his parents and saw hurt and anger flash in their eyes, especially his father's.

"It's because of you that my son is in that casket! You are going to rot in hell for all the dirty deeds you've been doing and what you had my son doing. I will not forgive you for this. As God is my witness, I won't!" Jerrod's father yelled.

Immediately, he was detained and ushered out of the church. His wife looked and shook her head with tears streaming down her face. She followed her husband as he was taken out. The whole scene was sad and very heartbreaking. One thing about it, God had a way that was mighty sweet.

As he continued to preach the homegoing message, Jackson had a strange feeling that someone was watching him. He couldn't pinpoint who it was because there were too many people in the church. His gut let him know that danger was around the corner. Jackson knew he had wronged a lot of people and had done a lot of dirt. He shook off the uneasy feeling and continued to preach.

In the back, blending in with the crowd, Marshall Lyndon watched as Jackson's hypocritical ass *so-called* preached. He was only lying and standing before God doing so. Getting shot and almost losing his life had done nothing to change his heart or his ways. It was apparent that God was going to show him who had the power. Jackson was still playing with God in His house.

Marshall wasn't the most religious man, but he did pray and read his bible. What he hated more than anything was for someone to use God and the church as a playground. He listened a little while longer before disappearing. Marshall turned around and looked dead at Jackson. Marshall smirked before walking out of the church with Jackson staring after him.

Chapter Fourteen

Camille was coming from the top floor of Club 404 as she looked around. It was packed on a Friday night, like always. She noticed that Andre would do a few appearances here and there, but since he and Summer were no longer rocking, he stayed away. Even though she was pregnant, she still tried to get her sexy on. Men flocked to her and she loved the attention. Camille had a pretty face, along with a nice body, but she also had a deadly secret.

Camille, at this point, didn't care whose life she ruined. Hers had been ruined, so it didn't matter. Ever since that night she was raped outside of Blue Diamonds, she hadn't cared about anything anymore. Her focus was revenge on whomever she saw fit. She was barely twenty-five and her life was gone. When she thought about seeing Lauren that day, she smiled inwardly.

So engrossed in her thoughts, she ran into a hard body. She looked up and she had to admit, for him to be an older guy, he was very easy on the eyes. In a weird way, he reminded her of Andre. Maybe she was tripping because she had been vying for his attention. The stranger held her at her waist as he smiled down at her. She could have sworn her heart dropped to her stomach at how gorgeous his smile was.

"I'm sorry, I wasn't looking where I was going. I had a lot on my mind." Camille flashed a flirtatious smile.

"That's cool. What's your name, beautiful?"

"Camille Jones. And you are?" She raised a perfectly arched brow.

"Marshall Lyndon."

******

Andre had just walked into his condo down in Miami. He had been there for the last day or so. Andre was busy making things happen because he was thinking about making Miami his home. He felt there was nothing but evil back in Atlanta. There was evil everywhere if he were honest, but for him, it was just too much. He needed a change of scenery. A fresh start would do him some good. Andre ran his hands over his spinning waves as he walked into the kitchen. The way his condo was set up, he had a view of the backyard next door. When he was there last, he didn't remember anyone living there.

He stood there, staring out the sliding glass doors. Just as he was about to turn and go back the other way, he caught a glimpse of a figure. His eyes widened when he saw it was Summer. She was still just as beautiful as the day he'd met her. Her chocolate legs glistened in her shorts. Andre had to bite down on his lips from the sinful thoughts going through his head.

"Damn...," he whispered.

Summer's hair was in its naturally curly state and it fell down around her shoulders. She seemed at peace, although she was missing the hell out of Andre and her mom. As if she knew someone was staring at her, she turned and looked right into Andre's light brown eyes. Her pulse raced and the familiar feeling between her thick thighs began.

Within seconds, Andre headed over to her. Her breath was stuck because of the intense look on his face. He approached her, towering over her. She had no choice but to tilt her head and look up into his soulful eyes. They were lost in each other's stare. It was like their souls were connected.

"What are you doing here?" Summer frowned, pushing her hair away from her face.

"Business and a change of scenery. Too much bad blood in the A. I missed you so much. I feel like God keeps bringing us together." He caressed her cheek lovingly.

Summer shook her head as if she was saying no, but she knew what Andre was saying was the truth. Of their own accord, her small hands slid up his chest and around his neck. She had to get on her tiptoes to do so. When she did, he lifted her, and her legs automatically wrapped around his waist and he held her bottom. He walked them over to her deck and took a seat with her still straddling his body. Andre pulled her down by her hair and kissed her with so much love and passion, she could have sworn she saw stars.

"I missed you so damn much, Summer," he said against her lips with his head resting against her forehead.

"I missed you too."

"Summer, God put us in each other's lives for a reason. We need each other and God knows that. Obviously, your mother does, too. I know there is a lot of drama surrounding us, but even still, it doesn't affect the way I feel about you. I love you, Summer."

"I love you, too, Andre," she told him as she linked their hands together.

They were both home. Home was where the heart was, and her heart was always with Andre, no matter how far away. It had been such a short time for them, but the connection was uncanny. The connection they had was like no other. What she adored the most was that it wasn't all sexual. They had a deeper connection, and that for her was very important. They fit perfectly, regardless of the flaws that each of them carried.

"Andre, I don't think I will be going back to Atlanta to live. I will go back to visit my mother, but there is nothing there for me anymore. I still love my father, but right now, I can't deal with him. God is going to have to deal with me on that level because right now, my heart is still hard."

"Baby, I was just thinking the same thing. You are my life, with the exception of my uncle, which I'm still getting used to. As long as we are together, it doesn't matter where we are," Andre assured her.

The rest of the day, they were wrapped in each other's arms. He showed her around and even let her know what his plans were for opening another club in Miami. She told him how things were going with her makeup boutique and it seemed that everything was good and everything was all figured out. The peace they felt was the best they had felt in a long time. As long as they continued to trust God and let him guide them, they would be all right.

******

Jackson sat alone in his home. In all his years, he never expected to feel like he felt. He thought he had it all but Jackson had nothing because he was too full of himself to realize he was nothing without God. Sheryl had written him off, and so had his daughter. Jackson thought he had the power to control the people in his life but God was showing him he didn't have the power he thought he had.

God was still displeased with him because he was still being the same Jackson. He was arrogant and still had a cold heart. Even his near-death experience hadn't changed anything. While he was in a coma and opened his eyes in hell, he made all kinds of promises to God. How quickly that changed once he was able to stand on his feet.

Even if Jackson didn't know what his next move was, God did, and God could see the turn of events unfolding in his life. God had given him warnings to take heed to, but he still had the choice of whether he wanted to listen and obey. Jackson was temporarily obedient when things were rocky, but as soon as it seemed things were good, he went right back to where he started.

"God, I don't understand any of this. I thought I was Your child and I know I have been faithful over a few things." He looked up towards his ceiling.

Quickly, his sincerity turned into fiery anger. "God, You lied to me. You were supposed to keep me and give me the desires of my heart. You left me by the wayside when You said in Your word that You would never leave nor forsake me!" His voice boomed with anger. "Answer me!"

Jackson was beside himself. He didn't like this feeling. He was having trouble believing that Jerrod had killed himself. Something about that had him on edge. He knew something had gone wrong or either something was troubling him. Jackson hadn't seen him in a while and that should have alarmed him. He thought of Lauren and wondered if she knew anything about what happened with Jerrod.

Tired of trying to get through to God and thinking constantly, he decided to head to Lauren's. He would probably get more information out of her. Jackson knew that no matter what, she would always be down for whatever. He smiled just thinking about it. Jackson grabbed his keys and headed out the door for a good time.

Lauren always knew what to do to satisfy him and ease his mind. As he drove through Atlanta traffic, for some odd reason, his mind went to Camille. She hadn't tried to contact him or anything. He was starting to suspect something, considering she was pregnant with his child. A DNA test still had to determine that.

A few minutes later, he pulled up to Lauren's house. He sat there staring at her house before shutting the engine off and getting out. Out of habit, he looked around.

Lately, he had been having these eerie feelings. He walked up to her door and rang the bell. A few seconds later, Lauren came to the door looking like hell two times over. The light she once had in her eyes was now dim with sadness and sorrow.

"What are you doing here, Jackson?"

"I missed you," he lied.

Lauren looked at him like he was crazy. "You shouldn't be here." Her voice trembled.

"Why? You don't miss Daddy?"

"Jackson, I'm HIV positive."

Chapter Fifteen

Before Lauren could catch her next breath, Jackson had his strong hands around her neck. "Bitch, you lying! There is no way you are HIV pos—wait," he paused. "Is that why Jerrod killed himself?"

Lauren blinked as tears pooled her eyes and began to slide down her face. Her tears were confirmation for Jackson. In a fit of rage, Jackson squeezed her neck tightly. Jackson squeezed tighter and tighter. He knew that if she had it, that meant he had it. Jackson couldn't believe the punishment God was laying on him. It was as if he was in denial of all his sins. His living a double life, trying to please God and the devil had worn him thin. God was a jealous God and nothing or no one came before Him.

Jackson kept choking her until she took her last breath. Her body fell to the floor and he backed out of the house, grabbing his phone. Jackson called his flunkies, Chico and Spin, to come handle the mess he'd made. Now he had more problems to worry about. If he was HIV positive, that meant he had given it to his wife. Sheryl definitely didn't deserve that, but then again, Jackson thought she was getting what she deserved for doing him dirty.

Jackson made his way down the road. Right now, his mission was to see what his fate was, but deep down, he already knew. Feeling even more angered by God, he didn't care about anything or anyone. God had betrayed him once again. Jackson acted as if he hadn't betrayed God and done his own thing.

Since he was well known, he didn't want to go to a public hospital or clinic. He would have to call a private doctor so he could keep things private. He had to find Camille because he had a feeling she was the culprit behind spreading the virus. She had been too distant since he'd last seen her. It was evident that Camille knew from day one that she had the virus and was on some revenge type shit. Jackson had something for her and her bastard baby. That Camille could count on.

Three weeks later

Sheryl stretched out on her chaise lounge. She had been a nervous wreck upon her doctor's visit a couple days ago. The doctor told her that he had found something abnormal in her blood work. She didn't know what to think. What she did do was pray and trust and believe that God would take care of her. As she relaxed, she thought about her life and how things had gone over the years.

Jackson had tried ruining everybody's lives but he hadn't succeeded as he thought. What did happen was everyone he'd tried to control had left. Jackson had lost his wife and his daughter. The very person he tried to keep Summer away from was the one God had sent her way. Jackson couldn't control what God had already mapped out.

Just as she was about to stand, her doorbell rang. Sighing, she got up and smoothed her hands down her pants. She really wasn't in the mood for company. Sheryl had a feeling it was going to be unwanted company. She swung the door open to find two policemen standing on her door. Her brows furrowed just as her heart rate sped up.

"Is there something I can help you with, officers?"

"Ma'am, are you Sheryl Jackson?" one of the officers with crystal blue eyes asked.

"I am. What do you need with me?"

"Do you know a Lauren Lyles?"

"Yes. What about her?"

"Well, ma'am, we have been trying to find the next of kin for the last three weeks, but we found that both her parents are deceased. You were listed as the next of kin."

"Okay. What is it you need with me?"

"Mrs. Jackson, Lauren was found in the Chattahoochee River. It appears she was choked to death, then thrown in the river."

Sheryl gripped the doorframe as she looked up at the officers. Lauren was wrong for the way she was living, but death was the last thing she wished for her. She actually prayed for God to have mercy on her enemies. "Oh Lord," was the only two words she could utter. Jerrod had been found dead, and now Lauren had been, too.

Sheryl wondered who could have done that to

Lauren. It was apparent that she had caused more drama somewhere and it had cost her her life. The wages of sin was death, and death was all around. She talked with the officers and answered any and every question she could. After thirty minutes of going back and forth, she shut her door and fell onto her knees to call on the Lord.

"Dear heavenly Father, I come to You right now, asking that You keep me and my family covered in Your blood. Lord, there is so much going on around me. Thank You, Lord, for taking Summer and Andre away from this wicked place. I know You have all power and You make no mistakes, Lord. Keep me in Your protection and keep watch over my enemies as they try to attack. Lord, I thank You right now for Your blessings and Your love. In Jesus' holy name, I pray. Amen."

Sheryl knew that if nobody had her and her family, God had them. Things were spinning out of control and it all linked to one man: Pastor Jackson Jones. She prayed that God had mercy on his soul for all he had done and was possibly still doing. In the midst of her praying and thinking, her phone alerted her of an incoming call. Seeing that it was Dr. Juarez, she said a silent prayer before answering.

"Mrs. Jones, I have the official results of your test..."

Chapter Sixteen

"Jonas, I met a really nice guy a few weeks back. He's an older man. I think that's what I need in my life right now," she told her brother with a smile plastered on her face.

"Who is this man?" Jonas questioned.

Camille thought about it before answering. Marshall didn't want anyone to know about him so soon, so she lied about his name. "His name is Nate Walker," she said, letting the lie roll off her tongue.

"Camille, you know you have to be careful who you deal with out here in these streets. I have done a lot of dirty deeds, and I know people are watching me. Then, on top of that, people don't know I'm your brother and I plan on keeping it that way."

"Damn, you act like I can't have fun. I understand there is a lot at stake, but I have my own agenda as well."

"Be careful because I don't want you to end up like Lauren Lyles."

Camille had been so caught up in her little affair, she thought her brother knew about her being HIV positive. "What are you talking about? What happened to Lauren?"

"She was found dead about three weeks ago in the Chattahoochee River. Apparently, she was strangled or choked to death before she was thrown in the river."

Camille stood there staring at her brother as if she had just been told something in Japanese. People were dropping like flies. First, Jerrod killed himself, and now someone had killed Lauren. In a way, she hated it because now she didn't have to suffer from the virus progressing. She was taken away too soon. Camille wanted to see her suffer, and unfortunately, she wouldn't.

As she sat there looking at her brother, that made her think of a conversation she and Marshall had. It was now nagging at her. There was something so mysterious about Marshall that gave her chills.

"Camille, you can never trust anyone. People will stab you in the back while staring you in the eyes. That's how good they have become nowadays. There are a few people who have done a lot of dirty deeds to cover up things that someone has done. The pieces are starting to

fall into place where they belong."He smiled at her, making Camille a little uncomfortable.

"What are you saying, Marshall?"

"I'm saying that no one can ever know about who I am. If anyone finds out, then that's my life. I'm trying to get to them before they get to me. In order for me to get them first, I have to keep a low profile. You understand, don't you?"

Camille nodded in understanding.

She knew Marshall was trying to tell her something, and now she wondered if he was warning her that he was going to kill Lauren. There were so many questions roaming around her head that she was becoming dizzy. Was Marshall Lyndon a killer? Something definitely was going on and she had to tread lightly with both her brother and Marshall Lyndon. Things were really not making sense. She had a feeling that, as always, Jackson had something to do with all that was going on.

"Camille, I want to meet this mystery man you are dealing with. I don't want to see you hurt by some bullshit that has ties to Jackson."

"Okay," was Camille's reply as she licked her lips nervously.

Jonas got up and walked out of the room. He had a gut feeling that whoever the guy was was trying to use his sister for information. Camille was known for getting caught up with a man. At first, she was caught up with Andre, and that was the initial plan. There was just too much going on and Jonas had to make sure he trod lightly.

******

Summer and Andre sat out on the top of Andre's restaurant, having a late dinner. She had received the news about Lauren and her heart hurt for her once best friend. Summer had plans to come home. Her mother told her there was no need because she was going to be cremated. There wasn't going to be a formal service for her. She wished Lauren would have done things differently in her life.

"Summer, you okay?" Andre asked in a concerned tone.

"Yeah, I'm just thinking about Lauren. I know we weren't on good terms, but it's just hard to believe she is gone. What's even harder to believe is that someone killed her. There are so many questions roaming around in my head about her murder. What was the reason for someone killing her? Then, on top of that, Jerrod killed himself a couple of weeks before." Summer sighed as she placed her fork on her plate.

Andre grabbed her hand, rubbing his thumb on her smooth skin. He looked into her eyes and saw the hurt and sadness there. He had a feeling that Jackson had something to do with Lauren's murder, but right now, he didn't want to voice his thoughts. Jackson was still up to the same shit. Nothing had changed. He was the type of man who bargained with God when his back was against the wall, then he would renege when things were all good or he was angry.

He hated that Jackson was causing so much pain even when Summer wasn't around. "Summer, I know you may be feeling guilty about how things ended with you and Lauren, but God knows you still loved her as your best friend. You were just hurt and that's understandable."

"You're right, it's just such a shock. I feel like she

was on a good path, or at least trying to get on the right path. Anyway, enough about that. What are we getting into after this fabulous meal?" Summer smiled.

"What would you like to get into?" Andre flashed a grin, revealing his dimples.

"How about a walk on the beach?"

"Whatever you want, pretty lady."

A few seconds later, one of the servers came and removed the dishes from the table. Andre stood and pulled Summer up from her chair, pulling her close to him. He took her lips in a fiery kiss that left her speechless and dazed. Andre grabbed her hand and led them downstairs from the top of the restaurant. People watched the couple as they walked through.

They made their way to the beach and walked hand in hand, looking at the night sky. As they walked down through the sand, they were lost in their own thoughts. Just as Andre was about to say something, his phone vibrated in his pocket. He stopped walking to pull his phone from his Robin's jeans. When he saw who was calling, he knew it had to be something important.

"What's good, Unc?"

Summer looked up at him as soon as the word Unc rolled from his lips. Summer watched as his handsome face became marred with a deep scowl. She knew then that Marshall was telling him something he didn't want to hear. The muscle in his jaw ticked frantically. Whatever it was, she hoped it wasn't anything too serious. The call ended and Andre looked out into the ocean.

"Baby, what's wrong? Talk to me," Summer asked as she gripped his arm.

"Camille is Detective Jonas Smith's sister."

Chapter Seventeen

Sheryl praised God because He had really been keeping her. When she had gotten the call about her test results a couple weeks ago, she was worried. Once she went in, Dr. Juarez told her that he thought she may have been HIV positive. After a series of tests, all her tests came back negative. God was an awesome God and she thanked Him over and over again. Nobody but God. She hadn't told her daughter because she didn't want Summer worrying and she didn't want her coming back.

Sheryl was headed to Jackson's home. She had some choice words for him. When she pulled up, she sat there and stared out the windshield. She wondered if he had any idea that he may have been HIV positive. Knowing him, he did. He was so evil and didn't give a damn about anybody but himself.

Deciding she needed to get out the car, she headed to the door and rang the bell. After a few minutes, he opened the door with shock evident on his face. "Jackson, I need to speak with you, and this can't wait."

Without a word, he stepped aside and let her in. He

watched as she walked over to one of the chairs and took a seat. He followed suit with his hands tucked in his jeans. "What is it you need to talk to me about?" He cleared his throat, looking at her.

"Did you have any idea that you were HIV positive?"

Jackson looked at her and his heart dropped to his feet. At first, he wanted to play dumb, but he thought better of it. "Why, are you the one who may have given it to me? I mean, it's obvious you and Jonas had something going on."

"Jackson, you know just like I know that's not true. I take it that you don't know if you are or not. If you are unsure, you need to go get tested because I have been and I'm clean. I do have to go back in three months to make sure I'm still clean, though."

He looked at Sheryl and thought that she was just playing with him. There was no way she wasn't HIV positive. If he had it, then how the hell could Sheryl not have the virus? Jackson prayed that God hadn't put that type of punishment on him. Granted, he hadn't slept with his wife—hell, he couldn't even remember the last time he had slept with her.

"Sheryl, I know just like you know that you have it just like I might. Right now, you are in denial. Then again, it doesn't mean you contracted it from me. I will pray for your health to be in good standings." He glared at her face, void of emotion.

"No, I don't need you to pray for me because there is no telling what kind of wicked prayer you may pray. I have trust in God. What I will do is pray that God has mercy on your soul." Sheryl stood and walked out, leaving an angry Jackson.

Jackson wanted to be angry but he knew he was to blame for the predicament he was in. Everything around him was crazier than it had ever been. At a time like this, he wanted to call on God, but he knew he would be more than wrong. He could hear laughter in his head and he felt the devil was having a field day.

Now Jackson's life was a mess, a mess he'd made. There was nothing he could do at this point. All he could do was deal with the consequences of his sins. It was apparent that he had met his fate and the devil was having a field day laughing at the mess he had made. Jackson might have had all the material things he wanted, but sadly, through all that, he had lost his soul.

******

"So, let me get this straight. Camille is related to Jonas and you got her all wrapped up in you? How that shit work, Marshall?" Andre asked.

"I'm just good like that. Camille is HIV positive," Marshall said, running his hands across his salt and pepper waves.

"Fuck is really going on here?"

"A fucking circus with a bunch of clowns. Jackson is the ringleader of the bullshit. I'm just biding my time, though, with this Jonas shit. He has a thing for Sheryl and he will stop at nothing to get her. I just hope I get everything squared away before it's too late."

"Shit, you and me both."

"So, how are things going with you and Summer?"

"Great. I just hope shit stays good between us. There has been so much drama, and from what you are telling me, there is still drama on every end. All I want is for us to be happy and have some peace."

"It will be soon. I already know that things are going to get crazy. Just make sure you keep Summer safe."

Andre nodded.

They talked a little while longer and Andre left to go spend some time with Summer. Since they had been back from Miami, they had both been very busy. He was going to make up for all that as soon as he set foot in her door.

Chapter Eighteen

Back in Atlanta

"Shit!" Andre grunted.

He was hitting Summer viciously from the back. She was so wet, you could hear the sounds of how wet she was. Palming her round ass, he looked down and watched in amazement at how her juices coated his thick rod. Sweat dripped from his muscular body as he dug her out.

"Oh, God!" Summer moaned.

"This don't make no sense." Andre slapped her ass.

Summer started throwing her ass back and Andre felt like he was going to lose control. He wasn't ready to nut. The way her walls clamped down on him was making it hard. Then, she was so wet and tight. Their bodies slapped together while she gripped the silk sheets on her bed. Andre felt so good inside of her.

"Shit! Summer, here it comes."

He filled her womb with his seeds as she coated his rod with her cream. He let off so much, he felt he had made a baby. He had been craving her body and she was the fix he needed. Easing out of her, he headed to the bathroom to get something to clean them up. When he got back to the room, Summer was asleep. He chuckled as he managed to clean her up. After they were both clean, he got them situated in the bed and pulled her close to him.

Just as Andre began to fall asleep, there was a pounding on Summer's front door, along with the constant ringing of her doorbell. He frowned, grabbing some ball shorts and slipping them on. Summer rose, asking him groggily what was going on.

"That's what the fuck I want to know. Stay right here and let me find out."

Summer rose up, pulling the sheet along with her body. Andre angrily made it downstairs and yanked the door open to find Jackson standing there. He frowned upon seeing him and was ready to knock his dumb ass out.

"The fuck do you want? Most importantly, why are you here?"

"I really need to talk to my daughter. Please! It's urgent."

"Nah. I don't need you fucking with her mental or heart any more than you already have. She's in a good head space and I don't need you fucking that up for her."

"You don't own my daughter!" He glared evilly.

"And neither do you. Now, whatever you have to tell her, I guess you'll have to wait until hell freezes over because you won't be talking to her."

"I'm going to die," Jackson said barely above a whisper.

Andre didn't say anything, he just glared at him for a few minutes. "Stay right here and I will go get her. Try some bullshit and you will die tonight," Andre warned as he shut the door.

He headed upstairs to let Summer know that her father wanted to talk to her. As soon as he got up there, she was slipping on sweats and a t-shirt. "What does he want?" Summer asked.

"He wants to talk to you. Although I don't like his ass, I really think you should talk to him." He stepped into her personal space and caressed her cheek.

"It has to be something really bad."

"Go talk to him and you can find out what's up with his sorry ass."

Summer nodded and headed downstairs. Looking around, she was confused because she didn't see him. With a smirk, she realized Andre had left him outside the door. Taking a deep breath, she opened her front door to find her father looking helpless and lost.

"What is so important you needed to talk to me?"

"Sweetheart, first, I want to apologize for all the things I have done wrong in my life. I haven't been the best. I did your mother wrong and I also did you wrong. If I could change things, I would. Now, my time will soon run out. I won't always be around because my evil ways have finally caught up with me."

"What are you talking about?" Summer scrunched her brows in confusion.

"I'm going to die."

"What?"

"I'm HIV positive."

Summer gripped the door for support as the words spewed from his mouth. She couldn't believe what she was hearing. If he was HIV positive, did that mean her mother was, too? Shaking her head as if to clear it, she looked at him, not knowing how to feel. In a small way, her heart went out to him, but then again, she didn't feel sorry for him because he had brought it on himself.

"Did you give it to my mother?" she asked through gritted teeth.

"No. She got tested and doesn't have the virus."

"Good, then I pray mercy upon your soul. I love you, but there is nothing I can do for you anymore. Too much has happened and my heart is still healing from it all."

Jackson looked at his daughter and his heart ached tremendously. He couldn't believe she was turning her back on him. Anger began to creep in because he felt Andre had turned her against him. It was official that his life had turned for the worse. Without another word, he turned and headed back to his car. As he got in his car, he drove away with tears streaming down his face. He wasn't feeling the power he'd once felt. He felt low and lost. As he drove through the Atlanta traffic, his car steered him to Sheryl's house. As he sat in her driveway, he thought about all the things he had done to her over the years.

He knew that if he had done right by her, he would have her in his corner. It was as if reality set in and it was a hard pill to swallow. Getting out of the car, he stood outside and rang her bell. After a few minutes, Sheryl came to the door. She took one look at his pitiful face and knew he was finally feeling the backlash of all the dirt he had been doing for years.

"Why are you here?"

"I don't have anybody else. Summer has turned her back on me. Everything in my life is fucked up and I just need somebody in my corner."

"Were you in my corner when I needed my husband to be there for me? Were you in my corner when I cried and prayed for you to do right? It's funny how tables slowly turn. God has got a way of turning things around. You getting shot and almost losing your life didn't humble you. It's sad that it took a disease to get you to see the bigger picture," she sighed as she stared at the man who once held her heart. "God needed you to do right according to His word. You got ahead of yourself and was living all kind of ways. You had a responsibility, yet you failed because your heart turned cold."

"Sheryl, if I could take all the things I did back, I would. I have lost everything and at this point, I really don't know what to do."

"Pray."

"God ain't gon' hear the prayer of the unrighteous."

Sheryl shook her head and prayed that God had mercy on his rotten soul. Somebody had to pray for him. Even when she really didn't like him, she still had to love him. Sheryl needed strength just to deal with the likes of Jackson Jones.

Chapter Nineteen

Marshall stood outside of Camille's door. He had to continue to play the role of a man who seemed to have her best interest at heart. She was on some grimy shit, too, just like Jackson and Jonas. Jonas was busy hiding his hands, knowing he was the trigger man behind the bullshit anyway. He hated Pastor Jones for getting the woman he'd always wanted. Jackson had a lot of people on his head all because he was playing a game where he thought he was invincible.

Finally ringing the bell, he stood off to the side and waited. Seconds passed and Camille came to the door with a black eye. Marshall frowned, wondering what the hell had happened. He had a feeling her brother happened. Jonas was on some other shit and he didn't care who got hurt.

"What happened to you?"

Camille just looked at him with sad eyes. She felt like shit and everything was weighing her down. All her lies and drama had finally gotten the best of her. Karma had come and slapped her in the face. The only person she felt she had was Marshall. What she didn't know was that he was just using her to get to who he needed to: her brother. She just didn't know that Marshall knew of her brother.

"Just had a little altercation, I'm fine. Come in," she said with a flourish of her hand.

Marshall came in and looked around like he had done before. He felt like today would be the day Camille would confide in him. He was going to be sure to soak up all the info he needed.

"Other than the bullshit you have going on, what have you been up to?" Marshall asked, staring at her.

"Just trying to stay behind the scenes. A lot has been going on and my bro—" She cut herself off once she realized she had almost slipped up.

"What were you going to say?" Marshall questioned.

"Nothing."

"Camille, you can trust me. What's going on?"

For a moment, she said nothing as she weighed her options. There was something mysterious and strange about Marshall but she did feel she could trust him. It was weird how she didn't know much about him, yet she was going to put her trust in his hand. He hadn't given her any reason not to. Taking a deep breath, she began to tell him about the things that were going on. She went as far as to tell him about her brother, Jonas, and the bullshit he had going on.

When Camille told him that Jonas was indeed the one who had shot Jackson and had tried framing Andre for it, he took it all in. What really grabbed his attention was the fact that Camille started talking about him having something to do with killing Andre's parents. There was a lot of shit that wasn't adding up. Marshall soaked up all the information and even showed some empathy for what she was going through.

"Wow. That's some heavy-ass shit. So, I take it your brother did that to your eye?"

"He did, but only because I threatened to tell all his secrets, which now you know. Just promise me you won't say anything," Camille pleaded.

"Your secret's safe with me," he lied.

Marshall knew shit was about to get deep and he was ready to see where the chips fell. The only thing that had him puzzled was the fact that Jonas was the one who had killed Andre's parents. He felt Jonas was just filling her head with random bullshit. He knew for a fact Jackson was indeed the one who had killed his brother but he obviously didn't trust his sister.

After sitting there listening to her story, he finally left and went on his way. He had to keep a close eye on Jonas because he was definitely about to do something. He just hoped it didn't involve his family. Pulling up to his home, he made his way inside to devise a plan that would for sure reel Jonas in the way he wanted him. Death had his name all over it, as well as his co-partner, *Pastor* Jackson Jones.

****

Jonas sat outside of Sheryl's house. He hated rejection and hated the fact that after he'd done what he'd done, she still rejected him. He thought taking Jackson out or almost out would make her come to him. Instead, she didn't want either of them. Jackson had fucked up, and apparently, so had he. He was going to get what he wanted or she wouldn't live to see the light of day.

He stepped from his car and headed around the back of her house. Jonas knew that she wouldn't willingly let him in, so he was going to help himself get inside. Hopefully, he would get inside of her. For years, he had watched as so-called Pastor Jackson had lived behind the church, doing everything under the sun to stay relevant. He didn't understand what true leadership of a flock was. Hell, neither did Jonas if he was honest with himself.

Sometimes he was too smart for his own good. He eased inside like a thief in the night. He was surprised that she didn't have the alarm set. It was dark downstairs as he walked through. Creeping up the stairs, he smiled upon hearing the water run inside her room. It was going to be like taking candy from a sweet little baby. He smiled triumphantly as he eased into her immaculate room.

This is going to be easier than I thought. He smiled evilly.

Chapter Twenty

Jackson stood behind the pulpit as he looked out into the congregation. After all that he had done, he still had the majority of his people following him. He hadn't been preaching lately, but after all that he had been through, he decided he needed to head back where he should have been all along. He had lied, killed, manipulated and so much more in his lifetime. Since he had finally realized the error of his ways, he thought it best to go back. He had repented and wanted to get back on track. Jackson was still harboring a secret that was sure to cause more chaos. Just like everything that had come out, he was sure what he was hiding would soon come out, too.

God was a forgiving God, and he knew that only God could help him. He had gotten so high and mighty that he thought he was the one who held all power. In fact, he thought he was God. Looking out into the throng of people, he felt his heart ache not seeing his daughter and Sheryl.

"I'm not going to use the line that we all fall short, neither am I going to use the line I am human. The things I have done was because I felt a sense of authority higher than what God destined for me to have. I went about everything thinking only of self. Nothing I did benefited others, it all benefited me. It was all about power, money, greed, and status. I wasn't living Christ-like, I was living Jackson Jones like. I didn't ask God to remove me, but instead tried to walk ahead of God," he paused, looking out at his people.

He could hear people shouting *Amen* throughout the congregation. As he finished talking, he asked the church to forgive him because he had already asked God to forgive him, although he knew he didn't deserve it. He finished up his sermon and let one of the other associate pastors bring everything to a close. Jackson headed to his study to have a moment alone. After doing much reflecting, he realized God had humbled him. He wished that he had been humble to begin with and maybe things would have been different. If he could turn back the hands of time, he would. None of it was worth it. He saw that now. The thing was, he was a little too late.

After having his moment, he left the church. All he wanted to do was have time alone. He didn't want to be around people. Once he was home, he sat in his study. Tears streamed down his face as he thought of his parents. He wished he could go to them, but since they were gone, he had no one. All he had was God. He now realized that was all he needed.

****

Summer had been trying to call her mother for the last few hours. It wasn't like her mother not to answer her calls. Andre was busy handling business at his club, so she really didn't want to bother him. She had to go make sure her mother was okay. There had been nothing but drama over the last year and things were still happening.

Once in her car, she headed in the direction of her mother's home. Thoughts of her father filled her head as she drove through Atlanta's traffic. It amazed her that after all this time, the things that he had done had finally caught up with him. She couldn't understand how anybody didn't realize what they were doing was wrong. He had hurt his mother and even her. Not to mention the damage he had done by killing Andre's parents. God wasn't pleased with him being a leader and not being able to set examples for his people. He never lived by example. Her father put on for the purpose of entertainment. Sadly, that was what the church had become.

Finally pulling up to her mother's house, she got out of her car and used her key. When she got inside, an eerie feeling washed over her. Something wasn't right and she had no clue why she felt that way. She brushed it off as not being able to contact her mother. Looking around downstairs, she made sure nothing was out of the norm. She headed upstairs and gasped when she saw how much of disarray her mother's room was in. Summer began to pray silently as she looked around. Slowly walking towards the bathroom, she eased inside and her heart dropped.

Her mother was lying on the bathroom floor, naked and beaten. "MOMMA!" Summer yelled as tears poured from her eyes.

She checked for a pulse and one was barely there. Grabbing her phone with nervous hands, she called 911, explaining her emergency. All this had to be a nightmare. She prayed that her father didn't have anything to do with what happened. She knew her father was going through some shit, but she hoped he hadn't gone as low as hurting her mother. Within minutes, the paramedics had arrived and they began to work on her. She had no clue how long she had been there like that.

Instead of driving her car, she hopped in the ambulance and rode with her mother. One man's sins were wreaking havoc. Her father only thought of himself. The fame and the power were what had him bent. He never realized the pain he was causing. It was too much too soon. Hell, they were still reeling from all that had happened. They made it to the hospital and the paramedics jumped out, rushing her mother in. They rattled off stats as they quickly rolled her down the hall.

With shaky fingers, she called Andre, and on the second ring, he answered. Hysterically, she began to fill him in on what was going on. He told her that he was shutting shit down and was on his way. Summer walked over to the tall glass windows and looked out into the sky. She began to pray to God for covering, and most of all, healing. Things were so messed up. Tears streamed down her chocolate face as she looked into the sky.

"Summer."

She turned and fell into Andre's arms. People in the waiting area looked at the couple and the love could be seen radiating from the two. They knew they had a lot of things to work out and get right, but along the way, they were figuring things out. He wiped her tears away with his thumbs as she looked up at him.

"What the hell happened?" he asked with a frown marred on his handsome face.

"I don't know. I went to check on her because I had been calling her and got no answer. It's not like her to not answer. When I got there, an eerie feeling came over me and I knew something was wrong, I just wasn't expecting to see something like that." She shook her head.

"Do you think Jackson had something to do with it? I mean, shit been crazy. He seems to be on his last leg," Andre said.

"It's a possibility," she sighed, running her hands through her hair.

As they were about to take a seat, a doctor came

out, calling for the family of Sheryl Jones. Andre grabbed Summer's hand as they headed to where the doctor was. It was as if things stopped and stood still. The words that came out of Dr. Graceson's mouth were foreign to her. There was no way what he was saying was right. She couldn't lose her mother. She was all she had.

"Noooo! What you're saying can't be right." Summer shook her head, crying hysterically.

"I'm sorry, Miss Jones. There isn't anything we can do. With the trauma to her brain, the ventilator is breathing for her. She was without oxygen for a long period of time. Right now, she is in a vegetative state. Again, I'm so sorry."

Summer dropped to her knees in pain and agony. Andre held onto her as her body shook from how badly she was crying. Things just seemed to go downhill. How was she supposed to live without her mother? She was all the family she had left. Summer knew she had Andre, but there was nothing like a mother's love. She felt like she was being punished for her father's ways. It was like it was a curse. The pain was worse than a knife stabbing her in the chest. She was so distraught, nurses came and got her. They took her to a room with Andre in tow.

"No! Please! I need to see my mother. Please!" she begged.

Andre helped her to the room that her mother was in. Before entering the room, they stood outside the door. Goodbye wasn't something she wanted to say so soon. As wrong as it was, it should have been her father taking his last breath, not her mother. It was so unfair. Andre squeezed her arm in a consoling manner. They stepped inside and Summer felt like her heart had stopped. In all her years, all she had ever seen her mother deal with was the flu or a common cold. Seeing her lifeless, hooked up to all kinds of machines, did something to her soul.

Slowly making her way over to her mother, she wiped tears as they freely fell. Touching her mother's swollen face, she bent her head and cried silently. Taking her other hand, she grabbed her mother's hand. In a surprising moment, it felt like her mother had squeezed her hand. That made the tears stream faster.

"Momma...I can't believe I have to say goodbye to

you," she paused. "This hurts so bad, momma. I wish you would get up. You can't leave me like this!" she yelled.

As Sheryl laid there, it was as if she went down memory lane of all the good times before the bad times erupted in her life. There was once a happy time and there was once some peace. Jackson was a good man at one time. Somewhere along the way, he lost his way. Her mind went back to their wedding day.

As Sheryl made her way down the aisle in her beautiful white dress, Jackson's heart swelled with pride and his eyes welled with tears. He couldn't wait until she carried his last name. She had already given him a daughter. He couldn't ask for more. Jackson loved her more than he loved himself. He would die for her if he had to.

Sheryl looked around, taking in friends and family as she was led down the aisle by her father. She had never been happier than she was in that very moment. Finally, her father gave her off to stand with Jackson. His father began to start the ceremony as they got lost in each other's eyes. The love was evident in their eyes. There wasn't a question about it.

When it was time to recite their vows, tears poured from Sheryl's eyes. Jackson's deep and heartfelt words penetrated her soul. Each vow of love, life, and commitment was said with conviction. When she recited her vows, more tears streamed down his face. From that day forth, there was nothing that would break the bond they had nor was there anything that would shatter the love they had.

"I love you, Jackson."

"I love you, too, Mrs. Jones."

A tear escaped from her eye and the machines started beeping like crazy. Summer lost it as she watched her mother take her last breath. Nurses and doctors had to take her out. They placed her in a room because they were going to have to sedate her. Andre couldn't believe what the hell had just happened. The pain Summer was going through made him think of his mother. That was a pain that didn't just go away. His heart hurt for Summer. He knew Summer needed him, but he had to pay Jackson a visit.

He prayed that Jackson didn't have anything to do

with what happened. If he did, shit was about to get real. He left his number with one of the nurses and headed out. He quickly headed out and hopped in his Range. He couldn't stop the silent tears that fell from his eyes as he felt Summer's pain. Jackson was going to regret all the shit he had done and all the pain he had caused. Even if he didn't have anything to do with what happened, he was still held accountable because of all the lies and bullshit he had already caused.

Chapter Twenty-one

As Jackson laid in bed, he felt like something was off. He turned over to find Andre standing over him in all black with a gun aimed at him. Jackson rose and leaned against the headboard as he looked at Andre. "I'm going to die anyway, so pulling that trigger will just speed up the process," he shrugged.

"You talk a lot of hot shit to be in the predicament you're in. On some real shit, though, Jackson, did you beat Sheryl to death?"

Jackson frowned.

"What the hell are you talking about?"

"Nigga, you funny. So you saying you didn't beat the living shit out of Sheryl and leave her naked on the bathroom floor?" He tilted his head to the side.

"Again, what the hell are you talking about?" Jackson gritted.

"Your daughter just watched her mother take her last breath because some asshole caused so much trauma, the shit killed her."

Jackson thought his hearing was failing him. Sheryl

couldn't be dead. He knew he had done some cruel shit, but she didn't deserve to die behind his bullshit. He put his head in his hands and cried. His heart was heavy, and it was broken in two. Sheryl didn't deserve to die. He put money on it that whoever had done it, had something to do with him.

"C'mon, why would I do something like that to her?"

"Why wouldn't you? You acting like you've been a saint in everything that has happened. Plus, you've hit her before," Andre stated.

"This time, I didn't lay hands on her. I don't know who did. What I do know is what happened is because of me. Everything I have done reflected on people around me. I have done so much dirt and wrong that doing right is like a foreign language. This punishment is worse than losing anything I have. Sheryl didn't deserve to go out the way she did. Her spirit was too beautiful and she was too beautiful of a person to go out like that." Tears streamed down his face.

Against Andre's better judgment, he let the gun

down and looked at him to see if he was telling the truth. He had lied and done so much stuff that believing him was like believing a hoe saying she was a virgin. His phone went off, alerting him. Andre pulled it from his pocket to see an unfamiliar number. Answering it while keeping his eyes on Jackson, he listened as the nurse told him that Summer needed him.

Ending the call, he looked at Jackson, not feeling an ounce of pity for him. Everything around him that was crumbling was his fault. Not saying another word, he disappeared as quickly as he'd appeared. Rushing to his car, he started and peeled away from Jackson's house. As he was driving, his phone rang and he saw that it was Camille. He wasn't about to deal with her. Andre had other shit to deal with and it wasn't her. He pulled up to the hospital and quickly got out. Pulling up his pants, he headed inside, up to the floor where Summer was.

He went over to the nurse's station to find out what was going on. After the nurse explained things, he went into her room to find her on her side. Andre eased up behind her, rubbing her back. She turned and looked at him with tear-filled eyes. His heart broke seeing the pain in her eyes. She had really been through some shit.

"I can't believe she's gone," she whispered.

"Neither can I. Shit is beyond fucked up."

"Where were you?"

Andre sighed. "I went to pay your father a visit. I needed to know if he had anything to do with what happened to your mother. In spite of all the bullshit he has done, I don't think he did this."

"Well, if he didn't, who did? None of this is making sense," she huffed.

"Nothing has been making sense other than us. Whoever did that is a straight up coward. Whatever shit your pops had going on didn't have shit to do with your mom."

"I wish this was all a bad dream," Summer said.

"I know. I hate you have to go through this. Life is so unfair sometimes and things happen that we don't foresee. It's hard trying to live through the things that cause so much pain. God is going to keep you and hold you. I remember you telling me once upon a time to let go and let God." He caressed her cheek.

Summer was glad that she had him around. She didn't think she would be able to make it if she didn't. Losing her mother was the hardest thing she'd ever experienced. She was going to have to pick up the pieces. She just wasn't sure that it was going to be today. Honestly, she couldn't even say when. What she did know was she was going to have a graveside service. There was no way she was going to step foot into Greater Emmanuel. There definitely wasn't any way she was going to ask her father to give the eulogy.

After talking to the doctors, they released her with promises that Andre was going to keep a watchful eye on her. They left the hospital and made it to his house so they could be in for the night. Andre held her as she cried silent tears throughout the night. He knew that when she planned everything for her mother's service, reality was going to set in. Andre was going to be her strength and help hold her up. He knew all too well what it was like to lose a parent. He had lost both, and if he could bring them back, he definitely would.

Chapter Twenty-two

Camille was a nervous wreck as she paced back and forth in her house. Jonas was on one. He didn't realize that she was home when he was on the phone, telling someone he was going to have to get out of town because he had hurt someone. When she heard who it was, she thought she was going to pass out. He had to be crazy as hell to even want to do something like that.

She had been trying to call Andre to let him know, but he wasn't rocking with her like that. In fact, he hadn't been in a while. She wondered if he knew she was Jonas' sister. If so, things were bound to get ugly. Jonas hadn't been back to her house for the last couple of days. She had no clue where he was or what he was doing. All she knew was that she had to get out of dodge before things got even more twisted.

A loud knock sounded on her door, making her jump. She was beyond scared. The knocking grew louder to the point she thought the hinges were going to pop off. Backing away from the living area, she headed for her room. She screamed when the door burst opened. There was nowhere to run or hide. When the tall figure approached, her face marred in confusion.

"Marshall, what the he—"

"Where the fuck is your punk-ass brother?"

Camille stared blankly, trying to figure out how he knew. She knew if he knew, then Andre knew as well. She wanted to cry, but tears weren't going to do any good. She hated that she had gotten herself caught up in this bullshit. The sad part of it all, she didn't know Jonas was going to go off the deep end.

"Don't be so quiet, Camille. I won't hurt you unless you decide to bullshit me. Now, again, where is your brother? He killed Summer's mother."

Oh my God! she thought.

"Wh-what?"

"Your punk-ass brother killed Sheryl Jones. Now, where is he?"

"I-I really don't know. All I know is he is trying to skip town."

"Call him," Marshall commanded.

The man before her wasn't the man she had met

earlier. He was different. His whole vibe was cold and pure evil. Something about him screamed dangerous. In a way, he reminded her of Andre. Something about his aura made her think that way. Marshall was such a handsome man and she thought he was going to look out for her. She still had no idea who he really was and he was going to keep it that way. Jonas knew who he was, though. He was just waiting for the right time for everything to come together. Soon, it would and Jonas would truly regret the things he had done.

After Marshall got the call that Sheryl had been hurt, and then later found out she had passed, he knew instantly that it was Jonas. The average person would have guessed it was Jackson because of his trifling ways. What Jonas didn't know was Sheryl had cameras installed all over her house. The reason she did that was because of the life Jackson was living. After seeing the tapes, his blood boiled.

"Call your brother, Camille, and stop stalling."

Camille went to her phone and grabbed it with shaky hands. Tears escaped her eyes as she dialed her brother's number. The phone rang and went straight to voicemail. She tried again and it went to voicemail again. She looked over at Marshall and he had a stoic look on his face. Gone was the friendly and compassionate man.

"Look, Marshall, I don't know where he is. I don't have anything to do with what he did. I'm so sorry he did what he did," she pleaded.

"I'm sorry too because you are guilty by association. So, with that being said, you are coming with me. If he has any love for you or any sense in his head, he will come for you. Funny thing is, he doesn't realize I'm like the Grim Reaper. Get your shit and let's go!" he yelled.

Chapter Twenty-three

It was the hardest day for Summer. Never would she have thought she would have to lay her mother to rest so soon. As she slipped on her black dress, she stared into her empty eyes. Her heart was so heavy. If only she could bring her mother back just to ease the pain. Andre walked in wearing his black dress pants and shirt. His hair was freshly cut and he looked good. He eased up behind her and zipped her dress.

Wrapping his arms around her waist, he kissed her neck. He knew what she was going through and he was going to be her strength. Reaching for her pearls, she placed them around her neck and turned in his arms. She wrapped her arms around him and basked in the moment. She needed him to be her strength because she was for sure weak.

"This is so hard, Dre. I'm glad you are here."

"I wouldn't be any other place."

She nodded and smiled weakly as they walked out, hand in hand. They got into his car and headed to the graveside service at the Garden Memorial. He held her hand as they made their way there. Her mind was filled with all the good times she and her mother had. Even though she was gone too soon, she was thankful for the time God had allowed her. It seemed as if they had gotten there too soon. She was dreading this moment.

There were a few cars there and they pulled along the side. As Andre parked, he grabbed Summer's hand and held it. Getting out, he rounded the car and helped her out. As they made their way under the tent that was set up, Summer felt her eyes well with tears. A few members from her father's church were there and she appreciated it.

Everyone gathered around and a lady named Mrs. Wilma Massey began to sing "Precious Lord Take My Hand".

Precious Lord, Take my hand
Lead me on, let me stand
I'm tired I'm weak, I'm lone
Through the storm, through the night
Lead me on to the light
Take my hand precious Lord, lead me home….

Tears fell from Summer's eyes like never before.

Her body shook as she let the tears fall. Andre held her up as she wailed for her mother. Deep down, she knew her mother was in a better place. After all she'd had to endure with her father for twenty plus years, she deserved peace. As Mrs. Massey sang, Andre felt those words and it made him think of his parents. He couldn't help the tears that escaped his eyes. There wasn't a moment that he didn't think about them. Seeing the heavy load on Summer's shoulder made him want to be strong for her.

When he lost his parents, he had no one to be there for him and that was why he had gone the route he had. As he looked around, he saw Jackson off in the back with a pair of shades shielding his eyes. It was evident that he was beyond hurt. Regret and guilt were one hell of a feeling. Sadly, Summer had lost both parents. Even though Jackson was alive, he was dead in a sense. The pastor began to say some words of encouragement and comfort.

After the pastor gave his words, the casket was lowered to the ground. Andre had to pull Summer away because she acted as if she wanted to go with her mother. She felt like she had nothing to live for anymore. Her mother wouldn't want her to live like that, but the pain was too unbearable. People gave her words of comfort but it did nothing to ease the pain. Only God could be the one to heal the pain.

As they made their way back to his car, Jackson slowly approached. Summer looked up at him with so much hate, it could have killed him. Andre knew she was about to spew some hateful shit from her mouth.

"Why are you here!" she yelled.

"Summer, in spite of everything, I lo—"

"Don't you dare say you loved her! If you had loved her, you wouldn't have put her through all you did. The tears, the lying, the cheating, all the women and the drugs. Using the church for a cover-up and acting like you were God." She wiped her tears.

"God spared you and I don't even know why. It's more than likely because of you she is dead. All your foolishness is what cost her her life. That should have been you, not my mother." She broke down and Andre pulled her away.

Jackson stood there helpless and heartbroken. He

knew his sins were the cause of a lot of things that had happened, but he never thought Sheryl would get caught in the crossfire. His heart was broken and he felt like he truly didn't have anything to live for. He was going to die a slow death and there would be nobody there. One thing he was forgetting was that regardless of his evil ways, God would be there.

God was stripping him bare to show him that he needed to trust Him and put Him first. If Jackson had done that, then things would have been better. Jackson turned and headed back to his car. Before he got back to his car, he was stopped by a lady he had never seen before. The words that left her mouth had him momentarily stuck.

"God will show you the way."

Jackson stared at the lady's retreating back for a moment and finally made it back to his car. He felt so unworthy, he didn't even want to call on the Lord. He was too dirty and grimy to even utter his holy name. Jackson started his car and pulled away from the graveside. He didn't want to go home, so he drove around aimlessly. As he drove through the city, his mind was filled with thoughts of good times. Happy times once upon a time. He wasn't going to ask himself how he had gone wrong because he knew the answer. Somehow, he ended up at his parents' gravesite. He wished his parents were still alive.

He stood at their grave, staring at the tombstone. "I really made a mess of things. My life is all messed up. I made some stupid choices, only thinking of myself. Being a pastor wasn't about me reaching and saving souls. For me, it was about popularity, fame and money. All I wanted was the clout of being something in the public eye," he paused. "The way I have been acting isn't the way you raised me. I lost everything that ever mattered. The pain is so real and I feel so alone." He wiped tears from his eyes.

A rushing wind blew around him and he felt a sense of peace. Jackson needed that moment of peace. Standing there a few moments longer with his hands in his pockets, he prayed silently. He pulled himself together and headed back to his car. As soon as he got in the car, he got a phone call from a number he didn't recognize. Hitting ignore, he continued to drive. The person called back several times until finally, he answered.

"What?" he answered.

"Now is that any way to answer the phone?" Jonas said.

"Jonas?"

"What's good, my friend? I didn't know that your wife had such good pussy. She's a fighter, too. If the bitch would have just listened and did what I told her to do, then things wouldn't have gotten ugly. Since you fucked me over, it's only right that I fucked you back," he chuckled.

Jackson felt a rage like no other take over. He was far from perfect. Listening to the sick bastard talk about how he had raped and killed her had him on another level. He couldn't believe what he was hearing. For years, he knew that Jonas wanted Sheryl. Unfortunately, Sheryl didn't want him. Jonas felt like she owed him because of what he had done for her in the past. As he thought for a moment, something told him that Jonas was the one who had tried to kill him.

"It was you?" Jackson asked.

"I was wondering when your slow ass was going to figure it out. Now that you know, I need you to do a favor for me. Since I'm leaving, I need some money wired to my account. You think you can handle that for me, or do I need to reach out and touch your pretty little daughter?"

"Motherfucker, if you touch my daughter, I will kill your dumbass. Try me."

Jonas chuckled. "I'm going to send you the information where you need to send at least a hundred Gs. Don't test me, Jackson. Shit could get real ugly," Jonas said before hanging up.

Jackson pulled up to his home, not knowing what to do. When he pulled into his driveway, he saw a man he didn't recognize, but something was slightly familiar about his face. Jackson just couldn't figure out. He was alarmed because he didn't know who could be popping up at his house like things were all good. Jackson eased out of the car, letting his presence be known. The man turned around and Jackson looked puzzled because he favored Andre's father.

What the hell? he thought.

"*Pastor* Jackson Jones," Marshall said.

"Who the hell are you?"

"Could be your worst nightmare. It all depends on you," Marshall shrugged.

"What do you want? I have a lot going on."

"Lead me to Jonas. I'm sure he will be contacting you if he hasn't already."

Jackson looked at him like he was crazy. How the hell did he know that Jonas would more than likely contact him? He stepped closer to Marshall and looked at him curiously. There was something about him that would make the average man piss on himself.

"He just called me confessing to what he did to Sheryl. He's asking for money."

"Good deal. Meet up somewhere with him to deliver the money and I will follow you."

"He wants me to wire it to him."

"I don't give two fucks what he wants, persuade him. If he needs the money, he will do whatever he has to do to get it. I have his sister held captive."

"Who is his sister?"

"Camille."

Jackson stood there shaking his head. Like he had

said, everything pointed back to him. He had fucked up in so many ways, he had gotten innocent people caught up in his nonsense. He had yet to see Camille since he'd found out about being HIV positive. Hearing Marshall say that he was holding her captive was music to his ears. He wondered if she was still pregnant or if she had aborted the baby.

He decided to take Marshall up on his offer. That was the only way he was going to get to Camille and also Jonas. Things were actually looking up. It was going to take him a couple of days to get the ball rolling. He was sure that Jonas would be calling him back because he was planning on ignoring him for the next couple of days. It wouldn't bring Sheryl back, but it would ease his troubled mind that was all scrambled up.

Chapter Twenty-four

Three days later

Since she had closed her boutique in Atlanta, she had nothing to do with her time. Summer really hadn't done too much since burying her mother. Andre tried to get her to do some things but she would always snap at him. All she wanted to do was be alone and be in her feelings. She lay in her bed, looking over a family photo album. Tears pooled in her eyes as she traced pictures of her mother with her index finger.

She couldn't believe she was gone. Wiping the tears that fell, she closed the book and turned over on her side. Soon as she got comfortable, Andre came in. He eased on the bed and tried pulling her close to him. Like she had been doing, she rejected his touch. The one thing she wanted, she couldn't get back.

"Summer, let me at least hold you. I'm trying to be here for you, but you keep pushing a nigga away," he voiced.

"Andre, you don't understand!" she yelled.

Andre let her go and stood from the bed. He

couldn't believe she had just said some bullshit like that. He understood she was hurting but her choice of words was fucked up. Running his hands over his waves, he looked at her one last time before he walked out.

He could hear her crying, and as much as he wanted to be there for her, he left it alone. She needed time to grasp the loss of her mother. Until she did, he was staying away from her. He knew what she was going through. She acted as if she had forgotten that he had lost both parents at the wicked hands of her father. Clenching his teeth, he headed out to visit his parents' graves. He needed to feel close to someone, and there was no better place than to be around his parents, even if they were resting in the ground.

******

After doing a lot of convincing, Jackson was able to get Jonas to agree to meet him in the next couple of days. He still hadn't laid eyes on Camille. He wanted to wrap his hands around her neck and choke the life out of her but he was trying to live the right way. Shit was beyond hard when all kind of shit was coming at him left and right.

He had left the bank a few hours ago and had the

money he was supposed to give Jonas in a large travel bag. Jackson had so much money but none of that money meant anything to him. Everything was mapped out where they were going to meet and he couldn't wait to finally get the privilege of putting a bullet in Jonas' dome. He hadn't succeeded in killing him but Jackson was going to make sure he succeeded in killing Jonas.

A knock sounded on his door and he paused. Standing, he made his way towards the front door and swung it open. When he did, he got the surprise of his life. Summer was standing there, looking lost. It was like she didn't know why she had even come to his house in the first place. Something had led her there. For her to be there, she needed to vent and cry or just needed answers.

"Come in," Jackson said as he stepped back.

She walked in and looked around like a lost child. It hurt him seeing his one and only daughter look so lost. He closed his door and turned to her. Jackson was at a loss for what to do so he just stood there nervously. Summer looked in his direction and didn't say anything for a minute.

"Tell me why you did what you did. Why couldn't you be a better man, huh? The things you did hold consequences. Innocent people were hurt and even died behind all the retarded choices you made. Do you know how it feels to lose the one person who was real and true? The one person who had my best interest at heart?"

Jackson was stuck for a moment. "Summer, like I tried to tell you, I loved your mother regardless of all the dumb things I did. I was so caught up in being who I was, to be honest, I didn't care what I was doing and how it hurt the ones around me. It was all about me until reality started to set in. I'm HIV positive, then I lost the only woman who loved me in spite of who I was. My sins are catching up with me. I also know that they hurt people tremendously. If I could take it all back, I would in a heartbeat."

Summer just looked at him, not knowing what to say. After she had said what she needed to say, she decided she didn't have anything left to say. As she passed by her father, he grabbed her arm gently. "Summer, I love you regardless of how you feel about me."

Summer stepped from his grasp and headed out the

door. Feeling a weight being lifted off her, she hopped in her car and went to talk to Andre. She knew he was at the club handling business, so she pulled up on him there. She got out the car and headed inside. There were a few people milling about and they looked up at her as she strode through.

She was wearing distressed jeans and a fitted tee with Huaraches. Her hair was pulled up into a high ponytail and diamond studs graced her ears. The staff knew who she was and didn't bother to ask her any questions as she headed upstairs. Once she got to his office, she knocked on the door.

"Come in," Andre yelled.

Summer walked in and closed the door, leaning against it. Andre looked up from his inventory list and leaned back in his high back chair. He stared at Summer and his eyes scanned her curvy frame. She was beautiful, and she was all his. Right now, he wasn't sure if he was feeling her. Looking at her a moment longer, he went back to looking at his inventory list as if she weren't there. For the last week or so, that was how she had been making him feel. Now he was giving her a dose of her own medicine.

Summer sighed. "Andre, I'm sorry for how I've been treating you," she said, walking towards his desk.

Andre still didn't say anything. He kept working as if she hadn't said anything. Summer became irritated and was ready to walk right back out the door. She walked around his desk and perched on the edge of it, rubbing over his waves.

"Andre, I'm really sorry. I didn't mean to push you away and I didn't mean what I said. This is really hard for me. I'm just dealing with it the best way I know how. I need you, Andre," she pouted.

He eased his chair back and pulled Summer into his lap. Holding her at her waist, he looked up into her eyes. He loved her so much and wouldn't trade her for the world. Rubbing his hand up and down her jean-clad thigh, he basked in the moment.

"Summer, if anybody understands what you are going through, it's me. How do you think I felt when I lost both of my parents? It wasn't easy, and to make it worse, I didn't have anybody I could call on. All I had was myself.

I was so lost, I forgot all that my mother had instilled in me. The pain of losing them caused me to forget that God was always there, even when I was out there on some reckless shit. If I had someone, it would have been easier for me. I was fucked up out there. Losing both of your parents at the same time was like my life had ended. So, trust me, I understand your pain."

"I know and I'm sorry. Taking it one day at a time is the only way I can pull through, and with your love," Summer smiled.

"I love you, girl."

"I love you too."

They sealed it with a kiss, and just like that, all was forgiven. Through all the bull, they managed to remain strong even with all the drama. Real love went through tests and challenges and God knew that they had been on one twisted rollercoaster ride.

Chapter Twenty-five

Camille looked at Marshall as he moved around the makeshift apartment. She had plans of sleeping with him and passing her virus down to him. She was angry that someone had given her the virus so she was messing around and doing everything under the sun just to survive. She worked, but she had gotten accustomed to men taking care of her.

"How long are you going to keep me here?" Camille asked.

"As long as I have to. You don't get off that easy."

"Who are you really?"

"Someone who can take you out. Now shut up!"

Camille sat there, looking at Marshall. She wanted to stab him. She realized he had played her the whole time. The only thing he was doing was using her to get close to her brother. Had she known, she would have looked the other way. Since she'd had an abortion, she couldn't use being pregnant as an excuse. She waited until almost three months to do so. Her stomach was poking out and everything, but she wasn't going to bring a baby into this evil world.

She had been calling Jonas and she could never get through. It was obvious he had blocked her. Her own brother had turned on her and had left her to possibly be killed. Marshall watched her intently as she played with her phone. He knew she was in a fucked-up situation.

"Funny how the people you think have your back really don't have your back. Jonas used you like every other man in your life, and you thought I wanted you. Camille, you are a pass around and you are down for whatever. That's not the kind of woman I would take serious or stick my dick in. You so caught up with money, you lost all respect for yourself and now you have to live with the choices you made." He shook his head.

Tears streamed down her face. For the first time, she felt the words he was saying. He saw right through her. Not having parents who cared and who had thrown her out at a young age, she vied for attention from any man who would give it to her. If she had a gun, she would probably blow her brains out. She really didn't have anything to live for. While in her thoughts, Marshall's phone rang. She watched as he took in the information from the caller.

"Come on, and don't try any funny shit, Camille."

"Where are we going?"

"Don't worry about it. Just be prepared for whatever. Shit about to get a little crazy."

Camille stopped walking and looked at him like he was crazy. Something told her someone was going to lose their life. If it were her, there would be no complaints. She wanted to be taken out of her misery. Marshall grabbed her arm and led her out to his car. When they were settled in the car, he pulled out quickly.

They pulled up to a building that looked like some old warehouse. Camille knew that for them to be there, things were about to get real. She was terrified, especially with Marshall's mysterious ass. Another car pulled up, and when she saw who got out, she wanted to piss on herself. Jackson got out, looking like he was ready to commit a murder.

Marshall got out the car and began to have a conversation with Jackson. She had no clue what the hell was going on. She couldn't understand why they were there. Did they kidnap someone? What the hell was going on? She could tell from the look on Marshall's face that he wasn't with Jackson's shit. Camille had never been so scared in all her life. Dealing with Jackson had gotten her caught up in all kinds of shit. It was obvious that Jonas and Jackson had bad blood. She was starting to think that was the reason for her brother pushing her to deal with Jackson. Shit was bound to get ugly, and she didn't want to be caught in the crossfire of what was bound to happen.

******

Summer was leaving Andre's club. She was ready to get back to Miami. Being in Atlanta was very depressing. She got in her car and started out into traffic. When she looked in her rearview mirror, she noticed a car trailing behind her. If she changed lanes, they followed. Her heart began to race and she knew things would possibly end badly.

Grabbing her phone, she dialed Andre. The phone rang and rang. She knew he was busy and had probably stepped away from his phone. She called repeatedly and never got an answer. After all the things that had been going on, she really didn't trust the police. Once she turned on a two-lane road, the car sped up full force and rear-ended her. She screamed as she tried to regain control of her car.

The more she tried to control the car, the more the car rammed into the back of her. The last hit caused her to go into a ditch. The impact had her dazed. As she gripped her head, her car door was jerked open. When she was able to focus, she looked up into the face of a man she had never seen. Grabbing her from the car, he let her know that if she made a scene, he would blow her brains out right then and there. Tears streamed down her face as she began to pray silently.

Just as he got her to his car, she felt something prick her neck. She quickly faded into total darkness. The stranger placed her in the back seat of the car and quickly fled the scene. It was a good thing traffic was light that night because, if not, things wouldn't have gone as smoothly. Jonas smiled as he pulled off into the night. Jackson was going to regret how he'd handled things over the years.

Chapter Twenty-six

Andre was putting out fires at his club. He made it back to his office to find that Summer had called him repeatedly. He tried calling her back, but her phone rang and rang. Andre called back to back and he still got no answer. He began to worry because it was apparent she needed him and he wasn't there. Grabbing his keys, he rushed out. He had to make sure she was okay.

Heading to his place, he hoped she was there. As he drove through traffic, he continued to call Summer but still came up with the same results. Once he was close to his house, he realized she wasn't there. He began to think of where she could be. He figured maybe she was at her mother's home. Turning around, he headed in that direction. He prayed she was okay. Andre wasn't doing the speed limit; it was a race against the clock. Finally, he arrived and his heart dropped when he didn't see her car there.

Right then, he knew something was wrong. Grabbing his phone, he called his uncle. The phone rang twice before his voice filled the line. "What's going on, nephew?"

"Something has happened to Summer. She's not answering her phone. I went by my place, then I went to her mother's. She's not there, either. This shit fucking with me, man."

"I'm in the middle of something, but I'm going to shoot you the address to where I'm at. Pull up and we going to get to the bottom of this shit."

"Say less."

As soon as he hung up, the address came through. Andre quickly made his way to the location. He wondered what kind of shit his uncle was in the middle of. There was no telling with him. He was always into something. Andre hoped like hell he could get to the bottom of what was going on with Summer.

******

"Canty?" Officer Johnson called out.

Canty made his way towards the vehicle. When they looked inside, they found a phone in the passenger side floorboard. He reached inside and grabbed the phone. Someone had gotten the victim out of the car. Looking at the phone, his mind began to wander. His gut was telling him that someone had kidnapped Summer Jones.

Johnson was about to say something when Canty made a hasty retreat back to where he was previously. He knelt down and a syringe lay on the ground. Right then, he knew something bad had happened. Now, it was just trying to put the pieces together. Canty gave out orders to get the syringe and phone to forensics. They had to get to the bottom of this before it was too late. If Johnson and Canty knew that Detective Smith had something to do with this, they would for sure lose it.

******

Summer awoke, looking around the room she was in. She was confused and still dazed from what had happened. Why was this even happening? She knew it had something to do with her father. Everything revolved around her father's sins. There she was, laid up with some lunatic-ass man because he obviously had some kind of vendetta against Jackson.

When the man walked in, she looked at him, not knowing who he was or what he wanted with her. The sinister smile on his face made her blood turn cold. She prayed that God got her out of this situation. He stepped to the bed he had her tied to. Caressing her cheek, he smirked.

"You are beautiful. I wonder if your pussy is as good as your mother's. See, your mother was somebody I thought I would have if I got Jackson out of the way. Your father betrayed me when he turned his back on me. If it had not been for me hiding his evidence after killing Andre's parents, he more than likely would be in jail as we speak. Your father owed me a lot more than what he gave. I put my fucking job on the line for him."

"What my father has done has nothing to do with me."

"That's where you are wrong, sweetheart. Everything that pertains to his fake ass revolves around the ones closest to him. By default, you will get the same fate as your beautiful mother. It was such a shame because I really wanted Sheryl to be mine."

"Y-you killed my mother?" she asked with tears in her eyes.

"I did, right after I got a taste of her."

"I'm going to call daddy dearest and let him know to say bye-bye to his precious daughter." He caressed her cheek one last time before walking out.

Her mother didn't deserve to go out the way she had. Knowing he had killed her because of rejection hurt like hell. Summer couldn't believe what her life had become. She prayed she made it out alive, but the way her captor was talking, she wasn't so sure. All she could think about was Andre. Tears cascaded down her cheeks as she looked around the shallow and cold room.

There would always be one thing that remained: everything centered around Jackson. His secrets in the pulpit had spewed over into her life as well as every other person who had lost their life. All she could do was pray. She knew God hadn't brought her that far to leave her. She closed her eyes and hoped for the best.

One man's sins could make things a mess. People getting killed and killing themselves all revolved around one man. God was going to show Jackson that He held the power and He was for sure going to break him down to nothing. What Jackson overlooked was God didn't dwell in mess. She felt in her spirit that things were going to turn around.

Chapter Twenty-seven

Jackson sat in his darkened room. Everything in his life flashed in his mind. All the lies, secrets and pain he'd caused ate him alive. Things finally hit home after getting that call from Jonas that he had his daughter. He was now going to have to swallow his evil pride and work with Andre and his uncle Marshall.

Things came at him like a ton of bricks. He had lost his wife because of his selfish and sinful ways. Now, he faced losing the only person he had left. He couldn't lose his daughter because of his torrid past and even present. Tears poured from his eyes as he realized how he had messed things up. Not only had he messed his life up, but he had messed up his daughter's life with his decisions.

All the senseless killing and bullshit he had done didn't mean a damn thing after losing those around him who loved him. All he wanted was for his daughter to forgive him and he wished like hell he could bring his wife back. Because of him, people were hurting and suffering. Living the high life while trying to lead a flock didn't work for him. God had been instilled in him growing up. He let the way of the world and all its schemes suck him in. He shook hands with the devil and made a deal that forever changed him.

While in his thoughts, a loud pounding sounded on his door. Staring blankly, he just looked at the door. The longer he looked, the loud pounding continued. Slowly getting up, he opened the door to find Andre and Marshall there. The mug Andre had on his face was enough to make a lesser man run for the hills. Looking at Andre, he felt guilt eat him alive for the first time.

"Look, nigga, I can see it your eyes that you on some feel sorry or guilt type shit, but I don't wanna hear nothing. This ain't about you. This shit is strictly about Summer. If it wasn't for that, I wouldn't be here," Andre stated.

"Don't look at me," Marshall said as he entered.

Jackson couldn't say anything because he knew he was to blame for everything. He could see now that the Lord was making him Andre's footstool and there wasn't a damn thing Jackson could do about it. Running his hands across his waves, he took a seat in his chair. Marshall and

Andre stood over him, looking at his pitiful ass.

"What's the plan?" Jackson asked.

Jackson listened as they went over the plan. He was all for it because he didn't have shit to lose. If he died right then, it wouldn't even matter to him. His life was over all because of the choices he had made. There was no need to feel sorry for himself when he was the one to blame.

Chico and Spin were at the church, handling some business for Jackson. They had been handling things for him for the last few years. When Chico's father was killed, Jackson stepped right in and was like a father to him. He would forever be indebted to him for that. As he waited for the person to show up, he began to look through Jackson's desk. He didn't understand what had made him do that, but lately, he had been feeling some type of way.

As he was searching, there was a special knock on the door. Chico already knew what time it was. Heading to the door, he ushered the person in, collecting the duffle bag. Jackson was into so much shady bullshit, it didn't make any sense. They were all going to hell with gasoline drawers on, and they were going to bust hell wide open.

The money was good, and Chico wasn't pressed about the outcome.

He set the money counter into place and began to take money from the bag. As he started counting, the man known as Shy spoke. "How do you think Jackson got on top like he is now?"

"What you mean how? The majority of it was passed down, then he worked hard to get to where he is. I mean, take a look around you," Chico said.

Shy chuckled with a shake of his head.

"So you don't know how shady this nigga Jackson is, do you?" Shy asked.

"Say what you trying to say, nigga."

"You ever wondered who killed your father?"

Chico froze. He looked at Shy like he had lost his mind. There was no way he was trying to tell him that Jackson was behind the murder of his father. He knew Jackson was a heartless bastard, but he didn't think he would do some shit like that, would he?

"After this drop, I'm done with his shady ass. Jackson don't care about nobody but himself. Until he hits rock bottom, he won't understand the severity of what he has done. He has been walking around here like he was Jesus himself. That nigga can't turn water into wine or make the blind see. Just think on that, and if you are still questioning what I'm telling you, go down to the precinct and you will get the answers you need."

Chico stared at the closed door as Shy walked out. His mind was going a mile a minute. If what Shy had said was true, then Jackson was going to pay for everything he had done. Taking the duffle bag full of money, he headed out. He needed to talk to Spin. Chico really didn't know Shy like that, but for him to spit some shit like that meant something.

******

Jackson, Andre, and Marshall were located at a spot in the cut. Andre couldn't believe the fuckshit Jackson had been on. He had been living in the moment, and now everything around him was crumbling. He had gotten the money Jonas asked for, but he had no idea Jonas already had his daughter. As they waited for Jonas to call back, Camille sat off to the side, tied to a chair. Everything was

175

blowing up right in her face. Trying to help her brother had caused her to be caught in the middle of some bullshit.

Her life was over anyway. HIV was soon going to turn into full-blown AIDS, so she had nothing to live for. Her brother had turned on her, and so had Jackson. Nothing she had set out to do had worked. If they killed her now, she wouldn't care. Her phone rang, but she couldn't answer because Marshall held her phone hostage. When he saw the caller, a smile graced his face.

"Hello, Jonas," Marshall said with a devious smile on his face.

"Who the fuck are you? Why are you answering my sister's phone?"

"Let's just say I'm the Grim Reaper."

Jackson's head turned around so fast once he heard that shit. He couldn't believe what he was hearing. A steely look flashed in his eyes as he looked at Camille. In his mind, he could see himself choking the life out of her. In a blur, he rushed her like he was on a football field. The chair fell over and Jackson kicked the chair. Her screams were heard, and that instantly put Jonas on alert.

He knew he was wrong for leaving Camille there. Jonas just felt it was better because he knew she would mess something up. It was obvious she had messed things up if she was dealing with the enemy. He was trying to find out who the nigga was. Was it the guy she had met? However, it was bound to be some bullshit. Jonas came back to reality upon hearing his sister's screams.

"The fuck is going on over there? What are y'all doing to my dumb ass sister?"

"You mean, what is Jackson doing to your sister?" Marshall laughed.

Jonas smirked as if he could be seen. The news that he was about to render was going to shut all that shit down. Jackson was on some bullshit. He should have been gotten to him so he could get the money and be gone. Having his daughter was going to make things better.

"Put wannabe pastor on the phone."

Andre stood off in the cut, watching the scene. One man was the object of disaster. He had caused so much pain, told so many lies, and so much more. Andre went and jacked Jackson up so he could talk to Jonas. Looking like the devil himself, he took the phone from Marshall.

"What!?" he barked.

"Is that any way to talk to someone who has your beautiful daughter? I wonder if she feels as good as your beloved wife did. May she rest in eternal peace."

"Motherfucker, if you lay a ha—"

"My nigga, you have lost your damn mind! If anything happens to my woman, I will cut your ass up and feed you to the fishes," Andre said in a deadly tone.

Jonas laughed like shit was funny. If neither of them played by his rules, then… there was no telling what would happen to Summer. Now the ball was in his court. Jackson had no control, and there was no way him calling on God was going to help. God wasn't going to hear the prayer of his unrighteous ass.

"If you don't get me what I want within the next couple hours, you can kiss your beautiful daughter goodbye," Jonas threatened.

In a rage, Andre knocked the hell out of Jackson. All because of him, Summer could be hurt, or worst of all, die. There was no way in hell he could bear the thought of that happening. He needed to find her and fast. Summer didn't deserve to be caught up in the middle of his bullshit.

"I should have killed your phony ass. I love Summer, and if something happens to her, I promise I will kill you," Andre gritted.

Jackson couldn't believe how his world was crumbling around him. Sadly, it was just the beginning of the end. He was living what he thought was the life, and now his life was pure hell. Jackson was a lost soul and, at one point, was trying to reach souls. There was no way he could reach anyone when he couldn't be reached.

"Jackson, Matthew 16:26 states: For what is a man profited, if he shall gain the whole world, and lose his own soul? Or what shall a man give in exchange for his soul?"

Jackson looked at Marshall with tears in his eyes. That scripture represented him to the fullest. Jackson felt he had gained the whole world. While gaining, he lost his soul. Jackson had made a deal with the devil, and now he was stuck in hell on earth. He thought he had power over God. Making a deal with the devil was what had led him to lose everything God had promised him. Jackson finally realized he had messed up and he had no one but himself to blame.

Chapter Twenty-Eight

Detective Canty looked at the information before him. He rubbed his tired eyes as he stared blankly at it. He had a feeling everything was linked to Jackson's shooting. In the past months, things seemed to be undercover, but now everything was falling into place as it should. The part that really got to him was that Jonas Smith was behind everything. He had shot Jackson and even killed Sheryl.

Then, there was information from murders that Jackson had committed. Everything was like a big maze. It was like they were trying to see whose balls were the biggest. Apparently, Jackson and Jonas had some vendetta. Canty always wondered how Jonas afforded some of the lavish shit he had. He now knew he was on Jackson's payroll. Somewhere along the way, Jackson had cut him off, however.

His only concern was getting Summer back. She didn't deserve to be caught up in the twisted web that revolved around Jackson. Once he had Summer safe and sound, his next line of business was going to be arresting Jonas and *Pastor* Jackson. This was long overdue. Soon, everything would be over and God would have the victory, as always.

Jonas was so dumb. Apparently, he had forgotten he had put a tracking device on his sister's phone, so they had what they needed to get Summer back. As they drove to the location that was off in the cut, away from the city, Marshall looked over at Jackson's pitiful ass. He looked like he was older than his thirty-eight years. It was like he was morphing into another person before all of their eyes.

God was a jealous God, and every being would for sure reap what they had sown. For Jackson, he had sown a lot of bad seeds. Everything he had done would come back on him. Marshall knew he wasn't a saint and he couldn't judge, but there was no way in hell he would even play with God like that, being in the position he was in. Jackson was to be a leader over his flock but Jackson couldn't lead a flea.

"What's with the tears, Jackson?" Andre asked with a smirk on his face.

"For the pain I have caused. Sorry won't mean anything to anyone, especially you, but I have to apologize for how I handled things. Your parents didn't deserve to die like that. I allowed the devil to get in my head and prey on my weakness. I was the devil's puppet and he was the puppet master. I should have been wearing the whole armour of God to fight against the devil. Ephesians 6:11 states: Put on the whole armour of God, that ye may be able to stand against the wiles of the devil."

"It's funny how now that you have hit the lowest point, you realize God should have been the head of it all. People don't fool with God until they need Him. In your case, you need Him more now than you ever did." Andre shook his head.

Marshall didn't say anything. There wasn't a need because God was dealing with him. Seconds later, they pulled up to a big-ass house. It looked like a haunted house. The whole vibe was creepy. They had to move wisely in order to bring Summer out alive. Parking away from the house, they scanned the area. Getting out, they slowly made their way around the house. Jackson was going to be the forerunner since this was his mess. If it weren't for Summer being held captive, and the need to get Jonas, he or Andre wouldn't even be there backing his shady ass up.

Jackson walked up to the door, knowing this really wasn't part of the plan. He had to do what he had to do in order to get his daughter back. It was all his fault anyway. Jackson beat on the door like the police. He was beating so hard, it almost came off the hinges. As his heavy hand came up to beat some more, the door swung open. Jonas stood there, shirtless, with a frown on his face.

"What the fu—"

Wham! Wham!

In a fury, Jackson two-pieced him. It was a blessing that he didn't have a gun or he would have shot him right between the eyes. At this point, he didn't have anything to lose. He had already lost everything that mattered. Jonas was so caught off guard by the blows, he had to shake his head. He spat blood from his mouth right at Jackson's feet. His eyes turned to thin slits. Jonas had a gun that was right on the table behind him. As he went to get it, he was stopped by the cocking of a gun.

When he looked up, he saw Detective Canty and Johnson, along with Andre and Marshall. He knew he might as well give up the ghost because the game was over. He was going down. Jonas smirked because he knew he was going down right along with him. As Canty read off his rights, anger flashed in his eyes. Jonas was trying to figure out how Canty and Johnson knew to come there.

"We appreciate all your help, Mr. Lyndon," Canty voiced.

"Jackson Jones, you are under arrest for the murders of Anthony and Marla Sullivan, Chico Dodd Sr., Lauren Lyles, and let's say a slew of other crimes," Johnson said.

Andre left them outside to find Summer. Everybody seemed to be caught up in two people who didn't matter. Heading down the stairs where he saw a door opened, he found Summer tied and clothed in only her bra and panties. Tears welled in his eyes as he looked over her body. She looked so fragile.

"What did this bastard do to you?" he whispered as he scooped her up in his arms.

He rushed out the door with her in his arms. Marshall looked up and frowned when he saw that

Summer looked lifeless, and without a backward glance, they rushed away to get her to the hospital. Hopping in the car, they pulled off, going way over the speed limit. Summer had to be okay or else there would be hell to pay. Andre put that on his life. As soon as everything was over, he and Summer were going back to Miami. That was their home now.

*****

Chico and Spin had ransacked the church. It looked as if a tornado had come through and destroyed everything. Chico watched as Spin poured gasoline all around the church. Striking a match, Chico threw it on the floor and he and Spin rushed out as quickly as they had come in. There wasn't a need for Greater Emmanuel to still be standing because there damn sure wasn't anything great about it. Jackson was the devil himself without the horns.

It seemed that nobody had learned a lesson in all that had happened with Jackson. Not just him, but others who were connected to him in some way. Everyone was busy taking care of things, forgetting that God would show up and show out in his time. They fled the scene thinking they had done something when God had already moved and worked everything out. Everything done in the dark would always come to the light. There was no way around what went on. The fact would always remain that one could run, but they sure couldn't hide. God sees all, hears all, and most of all, knows all.

Chapter Twenty-nine

One week later

Summer was slowly coming along. At first, she was distant and didn't want to deal with anyone. Never in all her twenty-four years would she have thought she would go through so much. The pain she felt was like no other. She wanted to believe that it was a lesson in all she had endured. Right now, she just couldn't find that lesson, or maybe it was the fact that she was too angry to care.

She and Andre were currently in Miami and Summer was happy about that. If she never had to go to Atlanta again, she wouldn't care. As she reclined on the large bed in Andre's room, her thoughts were filled with all that had transpired. It was hard to believe that one man, her father, had so many secrets, which weren't secrets anymore. Everything he had done affected everyone close to him. It was like a chain reaction.

She looked up when she saw Andre standing in the doorway of his room. Her eyes took in his tall frame. He was so handsome and he was hers. She was slowly beginning to feel at peace. Summer reached her hand out to him and he made his way towards her.

"You were right, Andre."

He furrowed his brows. "Right about what?" He grabbed her hand in his.

"That God put us together for a reason. Even though it has been hell, we managed to make it through only by the grace of God. We lost a lot, but we gained a love that can't be broken."

Andre caressed her cheek while staring into her eyes. If he had lost her because of Jackson's and Jonas' bullshit, he would have ended up in jail. She was his peace in his turbulent life, and apparently, he was hers, plus her strength. God knew she was going to need a wall of strength. He also knew that Andre needed someone to be his voice of reason as well as his backbone. Summer felt like in order for there to be peace, God had to remove people from her life. She hated that her mother had lost her life in the process of all Jackson's secrets in the pulpit.

"You know Greater Emmanuel was burned down last week?"

"What?" Summer's eyes widened in shock.

"That's what the hell I said. They have no clue who did it. They are saying it's somebody who was affiliated with the church. That could really be anyone," Andre said.

"That's true. I'm just glad that Jonas and my father are where they should have been a long time ago. Now that God has set him down, everything he has done will weigh heavily on his mind. He will have nothing but time to think. Most of all, the only person he can talk to is God."

"Enough about that. How are you feeling? You need anything?"

"All I need is you, Andre. You have been by my side when I was being difficult."

"It ain't nothing, beautiful. I know you don't want to step foot back in the A, but we need to visit my parents' grave as well as your mother's." He rubbed her exposed leg.

There were so many bad memories there, she didn't ever want to go back but she knew she had to because her mother was there. It still pained her that her mother was gone because of an evil man, or better yet, two evil men. She had come to the realization that God needed her more than she was needed on earth.

"When are you talking about going back?"

"Within a week."

Summer nodded.

"What happened to Camille?"

"From what I was told, she has been placed under suicide watch. Apparently, she tried to kill herself. She is going to end up in a mental institution."

Summer shook her head.

"What about your club back in Atlanta? Are you going to sell it or let somebody else run it?"

"I'm turning it over to the guy I had handling all the vendors. He has everything under control. I'm going to open a club here. In fact, I have already been talking to some people and things are in the works."

"I'm so proud of you. Through everything you have been through, you manage to handle your business."

"It ain't always easy. Every day I'm learning to trust the process. Most of all, I trust God. At first, the hate I had in my heart was allowing me to seek revenge. My momma always told me that vengeance is God's and God is slow to anger. Even with me knowing that I felt like I could do things my way and things would turn out right. After seeing how fucked up Jackson's thought process was, I quickly realized I had to let God be the driving force in front of me."

Summer pulled his head down towards her and pecked his lips a few times. He wasn't perfect, but he was trying to look at things in a different light. Summer had explained to him that God always knows best. Andre was growing spiritually, and that was one of the key factors she wanted in a man. She wanted a man who would allow God to lead them.

"I love you so much, Andre."

"I love you, too, Summer."

Everything around them might have been crumbling, but the love they had for each other was standing strong, and Summer thanked God for that. She thanked God for keeping them both in their sound mind. A lot of people didn't make it through, but they did by leaning on the Lord.

Chapter Thirty

Jackson sat on his bunk with his bible in his hand. He was turned to 1Peter 5:8 which stated: "Be sober, be vigilant; because our adversary the devil, as a roaring lion, walketh about, seeking whom he may devour."

The words penetrated his heart because he was weak in spirit and he wasn't in the word like he was supposed to be. He could quote scriptures like it was nothing, but Jackson wasn't living by the scriptures. He felt he was above God. As he looked around the cell, he thought about how life could have been different if he had done what he was supposed to do. Jackson had lost everything. He had no one. God had stripped him of everything.

"Jones, you have a visitor."

Jackson looked up to see a guard standing before him. He had no idea who could have been there to see him. He was one of the most hated men across the state. After he had made the news for everything he had done, he knew all hell was going to break loose. Standing, he waited for the doors to automatically slide open. He was being sentenced next week and he prayed his daughter would come and see him before. He knew that he would die before he completed what he knew for sure would be life in prison

The guard cuffed his hands to ensure he didn't try any slick shit. They made their way out front to where the visiting area was. When he saw who was waiting to see him, he wanted to turn around. He already knew what the outcome was going to be. Chico looked at him with a hateful glare. If he had known he was behind the murder of his father, he would have been gotten rid of Jackson.

Jackson took a seat, looking around the room. Chico stared at him in a way that made chills run down his spine. There was nothing but murder in his eyes. The deadly silence was killing Jackson, so he decided he needed to say something.

"Wh—"

"Fuck kind of shit you on, Jackson? You killed my pops so he wouldn't take over the drug organization you had going on. What makes this shit worse is you acted like a fake-ass father figure to me. All that shit was a front because you were covering your tracks." Chico looked around. "Look where that shit got you. Here all alone with nobody not giving a fuck. How does it feel to know your daughter doesn't want anything to do with you?" he smirked.

"Chico, I'm sorry. I wanted power and greed was the driving force. The more I got, the more I wanted," Jackson said.

Chico stood. "Make sure you don't drop the soap and watch out for Big Kevin."

Jackson sat there staring at Chico's retreating back. He knew that was a veiled threat. It wasn't a warning, nor was it just talk. Chico had somebody inside who was going to make his time there a living hell. The guard ushered him back to his cell. His nerves had gotten the best of him. He wondered who Big Kevin was. Then again, he didn't want to know. As he made his way back to his cell, he began to pray silently.

"Father God in Heaven, please watch over me and take care of me. I know I haven't lived the way You wanted me to, but Lord, just keep Your covering over me. Above

all, Lord, forgive me for all my sins. Keep my daughter in Your shield of protection. Even keep Andre. In Jesus' holy name, I pray. Amen."

Something in his gut told him he wasn't going to make it the rest of the week. He wanted to at least see Summer one last time, but he knew that wasn't going to happen. Death was closer than he cared to admit. He knew he was going to die due to his illness, he just didn't think it would be so soon.

*****

"Would you stop? We are going to be late for the reservation you made, Andre." Summer stared at him through the mirror as he stood behind her.

"I run the show, so we can be late if need be. This dress looking real good on you," he said, gripping her ass.

Andre had been all over her since she'd put on the fitted, red dress. It stopped a couple inches above her knee. Her ass was poking and she looked like she had put on some weight. He rubbed his chin as he took in her body. Summer was beautiful, and she was his and he was hers. He wrapped his arms around her waist, burying his face in

196

the crook of her neck. Summer smiled, enjoying the feel of being wrapped up in his muscular arms.

"You know I never thought this would be us. I'm glad we are here and I plan on us going further. You will be my wife and the mother of all ten of my kids," he grinned.

"Who popping out ten kids? Definitely not me."

"You are popping out ten kids." He smirked at the expression on her face.

She turned in his arms and got lost in his eyes. Everything for once felt so right. Her mother told her they needed each other and she was right. Andre had told her the same thing. There were so many bumps along the way. Through it all, they were able to stand strong regardless. She pecked his lips and she should have known he was going to take the kiss to another level.

Summer tried detaching herself from his hold, but Andre wasn't having it. He gripped her ass and deepened the kiss. She was like a drug and he was an addict. All he wanted to do was ease her dress up and give her what he knew her body needed. Finding self-control, he finally pulled away. After a few pecks, they got themselves together and headed out. Tonight was going to be all about Summer Jones.

Andre was ready to live his best life with Summer. He couldn't see himself without her. Andre was going to love, cherish, and honor her. The bible clearly states: "Whosoever findeth a wife findeth a good thing." Andre had found his and she was soon to be his wife.

Chapter Thirty-one

Marshall had done what he had come to Atlanta to do. After visiting his brother's grave, he headed to the airport. He was going to New York. He had business there. Marshall had informed Andre that he would come to Miami in a few months. He wanted him to enjoy being with Summer. With all the drama that had gone on, he felt they needed their time. Minutes later, his flight was called and he walked through the terminal.

A smile graced his face because things were great. All the snakes were finally getting what they deserved. He was thankful that he was able to help his nephew out. Andre finally got the answers he needed. That was all Marshall wanted and he was grateful for being able to help make a difference as well as being a blessing where needed.

*****

The guard at the prison was doing his daily walkthrough. As he made it to the end where Jackson's cell was, he shook his head and yelled for backup. Jackson's body hung from the ceiling by a sheet. He was there, naked, and looked to have been beaten amongst other graphic things. The guard almost vomited at the sight. Someone had killed him and he already knew one of the night guards had something to do with it.

Uproar took place after the news traveled about what had happened. Shit was beyond gruesome. The guard by the name of Thompson had seen some things, but what he was looking at right now was a whole other level. He was to be sentenced next week but now there wasn't a need. Finally, Jackson was free, even though that may not have been the way he wanted to be set free. He didn't get to see his daughter one last time before his life was taken.

Jackson had lived his life doing so much dirt and had never really repented as he should have. At the end of his life, he was almost trying to do right. The thing was, God had given him chance after chance but Jackson had not taken heed to any of God's warnings. The way Jackson went out wasn't God's plan. Satan was now laughing at Jackson and was on to the next fool who would be his puppet. Jackson knew he wasn't living a secret life. Everything he did, God was aware. Every thought he had,

God was aware.

Jackson bargained with the devil in exchange for all the wealth, fame, and power only to end up with nothing. The devil only came to kill, steal, and destroy. He was persuasive in what he did and many people, like Jackson, fell for it. Before Jackson did wrong, God would speak to him in a small, still voice. Since Jackson was gone spiritually, he had become reprobated.

Jonas had been through his share since being locked up. All the dirt he had done over the years, he didn't think he would ever get caught. As he looked around the cell, he wanted to kill someone for being locked up. He didn't like how things had turned out. God had sat him down and he was going to need Him more than he ever had. It was sad that people lived their best life but never put God first. When things were going wrong or looked bleak, they needed God more than they needed their next breath.

Exodus 14:14 states: "The Lord shall fight for you, and ye shall hold your peace."

If everyone who was trying to fight their own

battles had let God, they could've held their peace. Everyone was so quick to jump and do things their way. No one realized how it would affect others around them. If Jackson had let God use him the way God saw fit, he wouldn't have been a lost soul. Nothing or no one should ever be before God. Apparently, Jackson thought he could walk in front of God, fighting his own battles. Everything was moving by His power and His power only. Nothing or no one could do anything without Him and God was showing everyone that He was indeed real.

Thirty-two

Summer stared off into space. So much was happening all around her and she was beginning to lose faith and hope. She understood that the wages of sin were death. Even though her father had done wrong and they didn't see eye to eye, she still loved him. Summer was numb and her heart was so heavy. She mourned for her mother and father. At one point, she was a daddy's girl and Jackson could do no wrong, yet he had done so much wrong.

Tears slowly rolled down her cheeks as she stared out over the horizon. Getting that call a few days ago wasn't what she expected. As she stood near the lake with her father's ashes, all she could think about was how her father should have followed God. She knew she wasn't a saint and had things to work on, but Jackson was placed in a position where he was supposed to live and be Christ-like. Now she understood Andre's pain after losing both of his parents. They had lost their lives at the hands of her father and now his was gone.

Everywhere she turned, it was like she couldn't

escape the pain. Her heart was heavy and broken into a million pieces. Opening the urn, she spread the ashes into the beautiful water. She couldn't stay in Atlanta another second after her father was cremated. She and Andre were back in Miami and were near the ocean. Once her father's ashes were gone, she placed the urn on the ground. Summer dropped to her knees and cried out. Her soul needed cleansing. Her spirit was broken.

She felt like she couldn't take anymore. As she broke down, Andre shed tears with her. His heart ached for her. He held her in his arms as she cried from the depths of her soul. If it weren't for God keeping her and Andre, she had no clue what she would do. Things were a mess and she didn't know if things would ever come back together. Death was all around and it was sweeping through like a strong wind.

"Come on, baby. Let me get you home," Andre whispered.

Slowly, he pulled her up, keeping his hands securely around her as they walked back to his truck. He helped her in and kissed her forehead before buckling her in. He walked around and got in. Once in the car and on the road, he grabbed her hand and held it. He was going to have to carry her weight. Andre didn't mind because he loved her too much not to be her strength.

Finally, they pulled up to his house. He shut the engine off and walked around to help Summer out, then carried her inside. Leading them upstairs, he went into his room. He made quick work of stripping her down. He prepared her bath and helped her in. Kissing her forehead again, he made his way out the room. He went to shower in the other bathroom so he could prepare dinner.

Just as he finished everything, Summer slowly made her way downstairs wearing one of his shirts, her hair piled atop her head. In spite of the sadness around her, she was still beautiful as ever. Andre loved her so much and wanted to erase all her hurt and pain. She plopped down on the sofa, tucking her legs underneath her.

Andre was shirtless, wearing only black sweats. Placing some of his famous lasagna on a plate along with cheesy garlic bread, he went into his living area. He placed the food on the table and then took a seat. Andre lifted her and placed her in his lap. Kissing her temple, he rubbed her back in lazy circles. He inhaled her scent, enjoying the feel of her being close.

"Baby, I need you to eat something for me. Can you do that for me? Please?"

"I'm not hu—"

"Summer, don't do that. Eat something for me."

She nodded reluctantly.

He eased her from his lap and grabbed the plate of food. He began to feed her small bites of the lasagna. Once she had enough, she pushed the plate back. Taking a seat, he placed her back in his lap and they sat in silence. There weren't any words that needed to be said from this point. All Summer needed was for him to hold her. Nothing else mattered other than what was happening right then.

"Andre."

"What's up, baby?"

"Thank you."

"Summer, you don't ever have to thank me for doing what I'm supposed to do as a man, your man. I love you and I will do what I need to do to make sure you are good."

"I love you too."

For the rest of the evening, he held her. He held her until she fell asleep. Andre took her upstairs, laying her in bed, then went back downstairs to clean up. Andre was so busy telling her to eat that he hadn't even eaten. Her needs were put before his own. Right now, she needed him and he was going to be there for her.

Hitting the lights, he headed back upstairs. Andre got in bed, pulling her close. As he did, he prayed over them and for Summer. He hated seeing her so down and broken. Jackson had really done a number on everyone. Most of all, he had done one on Summer. Andre had gotten word that Chico and Spin had something to do with burning Jackson's church down but none of that mattered. Behind all the drama, lies, and secrets, Summer was left to pick up the pieces. Sheryl ended up dead, Jerrod killed himself, Jackson killed Lauren and Camille had lost her mind. All the secrets and fake praising God had caused so much turmoil. In the long haul, God was still at the head and would continue to reign forever and ever.

Epilogue

Eight months later

Summer stood, looking out at the water. Her hair blew in the breeze, enjoying the scenery. She and her husband were out on a nice yacht, a yacht he had bought a few months ago. Andre and Summer had eloped about two months ago. Summer was happy and her spirit was at peace, finally. Over the last few years, Summer had been in a whirlwind of hidden secrets in the pulpit, and all those secrets had caused so much reckless turmoil.

She never thought she would ever have joy in her heart the way it was now. Summer felt as though she had been stripped bare. Through prayer, faith, and staying in God's word, she was able to put things back into perspective. She thanked God for her husband. He had been a breath of fresh air and that was what she needed in her life. God had placed them together and he also said let no man put asunder. Andre told Summer she was going to be his wife, and now here they were, loving each other like God had planned.

"You are so beautiful," Andre said as he placed his

hands on her protruding belly.

"Oh, tell me anything now that I have put on this baby weight." She playfully pouted.

"You look beautiful carrying our son. I can't wait to meet him."

Summer smiled, placing her hands on top of his as they stared out over the horizon. Even though her family was gone, she was now building her own family. She still missed both of her parents, especially her mother. It took time for them to get to a tranquil place. Everything made sense and it was the perfect timing. It was all in God's timing.

Neither of them thought they would be living the life they were. So much chaos had taken a stance in what they were trying to build but God always weeded out those who were the problem. Sadly, Sheryl wasn't the problem. However, God had removed Sheryl so she wouldn't have to go through any more strife. Andre, as well as Summer, knew that there would be times of happiness and periods of sadness. They had endured it all. Through it all, they were still standing.

"Thank you, Summer."

Summer turned in his arms to stare into his light brown eyes. His hands went down to cup her bottom. For a moment, they were lost in each other's eyes. "What exactly are you thanking me for?"

"I'm thanking you for loving me and giving me a real chance. Thank you for becoming my wife and giving me my first of many kids. We are in this forever and there is no turning back."

"Andre, I wouldn't have it any other way. We have to negotiate on having a house full of kids, though. I know we have upgraded to a nice home, but still, Andre." She smiled.

"There is no negotiating. Like I told you a while back, we are having ten kids."

"Who are they coming out of, because they sure ain't coming up out me."

"On a serious note, I really want a girl and then that's it."

"That I can do."

Jackson didn't want them to meet, but he didn't

have any control over what God had already planned. In the midst of everything going on around them, they fought for the love they had now. It wasn't easy going through all they both had gone through. When they wanted to throw in the towel, God told them no. Every trick and stumbling block that was planted, God removed.

What started out as something scandalous soon turned into something beautiful. Summer and Andre were where God wanted them. He had blessed them both and was going to continue to pour out blessings upon them. Summer's mother and Andre's parents were smiling down on them. God had turned it around for the good and nothing or no one would be able to tear apart what God had put together.

"Andre, I'm hungry."

"Baby, you just ate."

"Well, I'm eating for two."

"Sum—"

"Wait! What?" he furrowed his brows.

"I'm pregnant with twins."

Andre was happier than he had been in a very long

time. He didn't know how Summer and the doctor had pulled that over his eyes, but he wasn't complaining. In fact, he was grateful for God blessing him with two kids. Life definitely couldn't get any better than it was at the moment.

"Thank you, Summer. I love you from the depths of my soul."

"And I love you, too, from the depths of my soul."

The End

Be sure to LIKE our Major Key

Publishing page on Facebook!

CPSIA information can be obtained
at www.ICGtesting.com
Printed in the USA
LVHW041658061120
670968LV00006B/997